They should be going home after dinner, Nick thought

He watched Genna suck the meat out of a prawn and his mouth went dry with memories she didn't know they shared. Watched her hands grasp the stem of her wineglass and remembered...

"I thought you liked the lamb?"

Is that what was on his plate? He'd forgotten. "I do."

She put down her spoon and reached for her wine. She sipped and swallowed, and he couldn't help but notice the wine glistening on her lips, could barely resist the urge to lean across the table and kiss her.

"Nick, I'm...I'm..." Genna took a deep breath. "I'm seeing someone else."

"Is it serious?"

She glanced up, and he saw the confusion in her eyes. "I don't know. I...maybe."

Nick was so jealous he wanted to commit violence. Except the man he was jealous of was himself.

There ought to be some kind of spectacular booby prize for what he'd just done. He'd stolen his own woman.

Blaze™

Dear Reader,

I'm frankly fascinated by sexual fantasies. Why do we have them? What do they say about us? How are men's fantasies different from women's, and why?

If I were a psychologist (which was at one time my career aspiration), I'd probably study this subject and write learned papers. Since I'm a romance novelist, I play the "what if" game. What if a very popular sexual fantasy—making love with a stranger—became reality to a woman who'd buried her sexuality so deeply, only the right man could set her free.

I came up with the title first—*Whisper*. I think a whisper can be just about the sexiest sound there is. When the right man whispers the right words, mmm...

It was so much fun writing this book, it literally just about wrote itself. That doesn't happen very often, believe me. I'm sad to leave the lush gardens of New Orleans and the scent of magnolia that were such a part of this story. And I'm sad to say goodbye to Genna and Nick. But I'm happy to pass them on to you.

Enjoy *Whisper*. Who knows what fantasies it may inspire?

I love to hear from readers. You can drop me a line at Nancy Warren, P.O. Box 37035, 2930 Lonsdale Avenue, North Vancouver, B.C. V7N 4M0, Canada. Or come visit me at www.nancywarren.net.

Sincerely,

Nancy Warren

P.S. Don't forget to check out tryblaze.com!

WHISPER

Nancy Warren

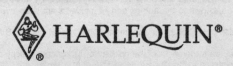

HARLEQUIN®

TORONTO • NEW YORK • LONDON
AMSTERDAM • PARIS • SYDNEY • HAMBURG
STOCKHOLM • ATHENS • TOKYO • MILAN • MADRID
PRAGUE • WARSAW • BUDAPEST • AUCKLAND

This one's for The Wild Writing Women
for being there every day with love and support and
sometimes a sharp stick. To Karin, Diana, Brenda, Caro,
Jamie, Kat, Catherine, Jeanmarie and the rest of the
WWW, my thanks. You guys rock!

ISBN 0-373-79051-1

WHISPER

Copyright © 2002 by Nancy Warren.

All rights reserved. Except for use in any review, the reproduction or utilization of this work in whole or in part in any form by any electronic, mechanical or other means, now known or hereafter invented, including xerography, photocopying and recording, or in any information storage or retrieval system, is forbidden without the written permission of the publisher, Harlequin Enterprises Limited, 225 Duncan Mill Road, Don Mills, Ontario, Canada M3B 3K9.

All characters in this book have no existence outside the imagination of the author and have no relation whatsoever to anyone bearing the same name or names. They are not even distantly inspired by any individual known or unknown to the author, and all incidents are pure invention.

This edition published by arrangement with Harlequin Books S.A.

® and TM are trademarks of the publisher. Trademarks indicated with ® are registered in the United States Patent and Trademark Office, the Canadian Trade Marks Office and in other countries.

Visit us at www.eHarlequin.com

Printed in U.S.A.

1

GENNA MONROE cursed the managing partner for choosing to host a law firm retreat in the most unbusinesslike city she had ever visited.

New Orleans.

The Big Easy.

Except it was *not* easy to be a businesswoman in this city that, as far as she could tell, treated laziness as a virtue. It wasn't easy that it took an extra five minutes to gel her hair into submission, fighting the humidity that teased it into a frizz. It wasn't easy wearing a suit and panty hose in the sticky springtime heat.

And the time it took to have a simple conversation!

She hated to think of the billable hours wasted here in the South just by the accent, those syllables being drawn out in that oh-so-relaxed Southern drawl till they begged for mercy.

Time was a commodity Genna took very seriously. She had career deadlines, a life timetable. She had no time for dawdling, drawling, Southern warmth and hospitality.

Give her Chicago any day. Efficiently cold in the winter, a businesslike use of air-conditioning in the summer. And no damned magnolias to drive a person to dreams.

Magnolias.

They were so ridiculously, over-the-top gorgeous, heavy with a spicy-sweet scent that made her think of romance. As did all of New Orleans, come to that. It was so extravagantly sensual, this crazy city, that she couldn't keep her thoughts straight.

Every sense prickled, as though each of them was waking from hibernation, as she leaned over the curly wrought-iron railing and drank in the beauty of the night. She gazed into the walled garden tangled with dark-green vines that flirted with moonlit statues, wrapping coy arms round their stone shoulders.

Behind her, inside the hotel ballroom, she heard the drone of more than a hundred lawyers and law-firm employees talking, arguing, schmoozing—just as she should be. Like they didn't do enough of that back in Chicago seventy hours a week. But ahead of her was the soft sound of water trickling from an unseen fountain, soothing and somehow cooling to her overheated imagination.

Her nostrils twitched as she breathed deeply of a heady combination of scents, only a few of which she could identify. Magnolia hung heaviest, mixed with lighter notes. Jasmine, she was certain; rose; some kind of sharper scent, maybe an herb. Even the earth smelled rich and fruitful. Warm, heavy, moist air pulled at her with caressing fingers, urging her to step out into the garden.

She glanced back through the lighted doorway where clusters of lawyers swarmed. Would anyone even notice she was gone?

In her navy cotton dress she'd blend right into the deep shadows of the garden. She stepped down one shallow stone step, then another, and finally another, with each step feeling her breath come easier and the surface irritability she'd tried to ignore all day deepen into a kind of sadness.

Why was she here, in this romantic garden, alone?

She wandered, pensive and frustrated, pausing to touch a waxy green leaf here, to inhale a fragrant blossom there. The unfamiliar taste of a mint julep was still on her tongue, as foreign as this feeling of dissatisfaction.

She was on track to being the youngest lawyer ever to make partner at Donne, Green and Raddison. She had the world by the tail.

She sighed and sank to a stone bench, sheltered under a cloud of fragrant, creamy magnolia blossoms. Giving in to their spell, she shut her mind off and let her senses take over.

The air was as moist and heavy as a kiss. The scent so pure and sweet she wanted to weep. The night sounds were so exotic she held herself still, as though she could become as much a part of this garden as the statue of Aphrodite, whose stone smile mocked her from across a twisting, shadowed pathway.

Above her glowed the moon, a heavy gold ring surrounded by stars as bold and sparkly as costume jewelry. The gaudy sky suited the energy of this city that always seemed to be preparing to party, partying, or cleaning up from a party.

And, for the moment, Genna was tired of the party. For a woman who was always in a rush, it was wonderful just to sit still. Not to think, plan, research or argue—just to be. She closed her eyes, letting her muscles relax and her senses indulge.

"Tell me what you want." The whisper was husky, masculine and as sinfully rich as bourbon.

Tell me what you want. Had the voice come out of her psyche? What was the answer? Did she even know?

"Tell me." Intimate and assured, the whisper wasn't coming from inside her, but somewhere very near. Goose bumps danced over her flesh, but Genna held her eyes tightly shut.

The lawyer in her pondered the import of that question. She could open her eyes and find a waiter asking about a drink order. It could be her best friend and fellow lawyer, Nick, suggesting they go to a jazz club.

Or it could be a mystery lover. She smiled at the absurdity of that last one. There was nothing mysterious about her love life these days—it was as null and void as a bounced check.

This time-sucking romantic atmosphere must be getting to her. She'd best go back to the reception. Filling her lungs once more with fragrant air, she slowly lifted her eyelids.

"I want you to make love to me." This voice was female, decidedly sultry and lilted with a Spanish accent.

Genna's eyes flew open. She heard rustling behind her and the unmistakable sound of kissing. Deep, wet, hungry kissing. It was coming from right behind her, on the other side of the bush that sheltered her.

The man's whisper held a hint of humor as he answered. "Your note hinted as much."

"Were you insulted?"

"Intrigued. You're beautiful." There was an undeniable sexual rhythm to the conversation between these two strangers that fascinated Genna. They used words like kisses.

"So are you." The foreign woman laughed softly. "I saw you and I thought, 'That is a man who knows how to please a woman.'"

"I do my best."

More kissing. She heard bodies shifting and three or four white petals drifted onto her navy skirt while she sat, rigid with embarrassment, and yet so enthralled by what she heard she couldn't move.

"It is only for tonight, *querido*. Tomorrow I must leave."

Were they seriously going to do it right there? In the garden? A few leaves and branches away from Genna?

There was a pause, and sudden stillness. "Are you married?"

The woman laughed softly. "A moral man. How unusual. No. I'm not married…anymore. I prefer my freedom."

"Good. So do I," replied that seductive, whispering masculine voice. "We'll make it a night to remember."

Genna leaned back slightly, wishing he'd recite poetry or something, anything to keep him talking. His whispering voice fascinated her, made her feel things…

She shifted on the stone bench as the kissing noises resumed. For now, at least, the erotic voice was silent.

Just as she should silence her own longings and leave. She glanced left and right, but there was no way out of here without going past the amorous couple. And she was getting a horrible suspicion that the situation was about to get a whole lot steamier.

"Your neck is beautiful. Your throat is beautiful... I want to see all your beauty. I want to make love to you under the stars."

Genna gnawed her lip. If she left now it would be awkward, but at least she would give them some privacy.

She heard a breathy sigh and realized if she waited much longer it would be too late. She'd better go now and try to slip quietly past them. At least they were still clothed. She half rose.

"Your breasts are as gold as the moon." The man's husky whisper had her sitting down again so fast she jammed her tailbone on the bench. Looked like they'd passed the fully clothed stage, and she'd passed the walking-away stage. She'd just ignore them and think about something else.

Let's see, there was that brief she had to prepare on the quantum of damages for a female CEO harassed by the chairman of her board of directors.

"Your skin tastes like peaches," he whispered. From the sound of things, he was pretty much gorging himself.

"Mmm."

"Lean back. That's good. I'm going to put my tongue on your nipples and when they are very wet I'm going watch them tighten as the breeze blows them dry."

Genna's mouth went dry and she felt her own nipples tighten. No man had ever worshipped her body that way. Maybe if they had she wouldn't have given up on sex as a big waste of time. What would it be like to have the whispering stranger treat her body with such reverence? What if it were her breast he was sucking? Her making those breathy moans of delight?

"Do you like this?"

Damned if her head didn't nod of its own volition. Her nipples tingled as she imagined the stranger licking them, this man who knew how to please a woman. She almost felt the soft air teasing them dry like a second caress.

He whispered endearments, earthy pleasure words, some muffled as though his lips were against the woman's skin. She was certain she even heard the sigh of flesh rubbing against flesh. Her body, denied sex for so long, quivered with vicarious pleasure.

"Spread your legs," he commanded.

Genna's knees slipped away from each other, without any message from her brain, as though her thinking being had separated from her feeling side. She felt odd: light-headed and so bemused by the real-life fantasy in this exotic garden that she seemed to have lost her will. Perhaps it was an enchanted garden— or perhaps she'd fallen asleep and was dreaming.

"The skin of your thighs is so soft. It's like silk. Warm silk." A sultry breeze wafted beneath Genna's skirt and caressed her. It felt cool where she was squirmingly hot, and she dimly recognized that her panties were wet.

"Do you know where I want to touch you next?"

"Yes, oh, please."

She heard a soft chuckle. "Don't be too eager. Hold your hips still and spread your legs wider for me."

The woman's low words were in Spanish. Genna didn't know what they meant, but they sounded desperate. Then the unseen woman gasped and Genna knew he was touching her, stroking her. Her body reacted as though it were Genna herself he touched and stroked.

"You're so wet." His voice was softer than the breeze. "Are you wet for me?"

"*Sí, querido, sí,*" the foreign woman all but sobbed.

Yes, oh, yes, Genna silently echoed, clamping her legs together as though she could control the throbbing at her core.

"This is a very pretty thong, but I think it needs to come off. Lift your hips for me."

"Hurry. I'm burning."

Genna knew just how she felt.

"You're beautiful. In a moment I'm going to bury myself inside you, but for now I just want to look at your lovely body spread out under the stars."

A strangled gurgle met his words.

"I want to feel you come. Will you come for me when I'm moving deep inside your body?" She heard the slide of a zipper. His? Her hands flexed with longing to touch his hardness.

"You know I will. I want you so."

Genna bit down hard on her lip to keep from crying out as excitement built inside her. She could almost feel him, big and hard and purposeful, filling all her hidden places, fulfilling all her secret fantasies.

"I'm going to make you scream with pleasure," he promised softly.

Genna's fingers dug into the rough stone, but she

couldn't control herself. Just like that, the sensuality she'd ignored for too long took over her body. She shattered, pressing her lips hard together to hold back her cry.

Trembling with a mixture of shame and excitement, Genna sat there, stunned, trying to control her breathing. Behind her she heard a tearing sound. A condom package ripping open?

"Hurry, please!" The woman didn't bother to whisper, and her singsong voice held an edge of desperation. "I need you inside me. Now."

"Anna-Maria? Anna-Mari-ia." An older woman's voice broke the magic spell of the night.

More white petals rained down on Genna as a frantic scuffling took place behind her. A string of low-voiced Spanish curses followed. "I am sorry. I must go."

"I'll come to your room—"

"No."

"You come to—"

"No. That's the flight attendant in charge. My…my boss. If she's looking for me it means our flight has been moved up. We will be leaving very soon. I am so sorry, *querido*. It would have been magnificent. Goodbye."

Genna heard one more quick kiss, then more rustling. A moment later, the woman left.

Then she heard another sound.

A very Anglo-Saxon curse.

It might have been amusing if she didn't know firsthand how frustrated the stranger must be feeling. She heard his breathing, harsh and ragged, and remained frozen in place, all but holding her breath so as not to be discovered eavesdropping. She felt like the unseen partner in a bizarre ménage à trois. She hadn't meant to listen, but it shamed her all the same.

She waited fifteen minutes by her flawlessly accurate Rolex before she moved. The man had left not long after the woman, so she'd had some time alone. Apart from the fact that she didn't want either of the parties in the arrested love tryst to see her, she needed to compose herself.

She crossed her legs and smoothed the skirt of her dress back over her knees. What had just happened? Was she that desperate? That needy, that simply overhearing another couple making love was enough to send her over the edge? Where was the self-control she prided herself on? The cool satirical persona she showed the world?

She was nothing but a sex-starved shell of a woman—as dried out as an old law book. She'd just had the best sexual experience of all three decades of her life—and she was an invisible partner. An unnoticed third wheel.

A voyeur!

Breathing deeply and deliberately, she resolved to forget the whole incident. But her arousal teased her like the soft breeze, taunted her as exotically as the scent of magnolia.

Something about the way he'd whispered, the things he'd promised, had spoken to her deepest desires. Maybe he'd been whispering to another woman, but she'd heard him in the most secret part of herself and felt as strongly connected to him as if they were lovers.

She didn't have a clue who he was. He didn't know

she existed. And she wanted him like she'd never wanted anything in her life.

When she felt cool and composed enough to stand, she forced her steps back to the verandah, vowing to forget the whole shameful episode.

Just as she reached the edge of the garden, she glanced up and her heart lurched to a stop. A solitary man stood there. A dark silhouette. Tall, broad-shouldered, he lounged with his elbows on the railing and she could have sworn he was watching her.

He raised one hand and she took a quick step backward before identifying the red glow of a cigar tip. She thought she saw his eyes reflect the gleam, as if he were a predator in a dark jungle.

Then she gazed beyond him to the lighted ballroom where the schmoozefest was still in full swing. *For goodness sake, pull yourself together, woman.* He was a colleague enjoying a quiet smoke on the balcony.

She stepped forward.

He was definitely watching her.

She stalled, one foot on the bottom step, staring back, her heart beating again in crazy thuds as her skin began to prickle.

It was him. She was certain of it. Some inner instinct felt the knowledge and held her frozen in place, staring up at the dark shape as a combination of fear and longing uncurled inside her. She drew in a ragged breath and caught the heavy fragrance of cigar smoke.

"Genna, it's me." The man moved toward her and his familiar voice broke the spell.

Relief flooded her body, along with a tiny pang of disappointment. "Nick! You startled me." She forced a grin and took a deep breath to still the trembling in her body. "How come you're not at the party?"

He gestured to his cigar. "Came to sneak a puff."

"Since when do you smoke?" She'd known him for four years, odd she'd never seen him smoking before.

He shrugged. "Not often. It was an excuse to get away from the noise."

"Aren't you supposed to be socializing with your colleagues?"

"You're a colleague." He gestured to a wicker love seat in a shadowy corner. "Join me."

She hesitated. "How long have you been out here?"

"A few minutes."

"Did you...see anyone else come up from the garden?"

There was a short pause. He glanced at her, but it was too dark to read his expression. She hoped it was also too dark for him to see her blush. "Not while I've been out here," he said.

Damn. She was hoping Nick had seen the woman and man she'd overheard. He'd describe them in all their sleazy one-night-stand glory. She'd amuse him with an exaggerated recounting of the frustrated love affair—editing out her own response—and they'd both laugh. End of story. Except he hadn't seen them, so the story wasn't over yet for her.

"Want a drink?"

She considered the offer. Nick was easy company: fun to be with, intelligent and always up for an argument, on pretty much any subject. But she was too shaken to sit out here chatting as though her whole world hadn't just rocked on its axis. "No, thanks."

He hesitated, seeming unusually sombre in the half-light. "Something bothering you?"

Again, she hesitated. Now that her best friend, Marcy, was married and the mother of two small kids, they didn't see each other much. Which left Nick, the man Marcy had almost married, as probably Genna's best friend. But this wasn't something she wanted to talk about with Nick. It was too personal, she felt too raw. "No. I think I'll go back to the party." She forced a cocky smile. "I have to get schmoozing if I want to beat your record as the youngest associate ever to make partner."

He chuckled softly. "Knock yourself out."

She took a step away, but Nick stopped her with a hand on her arm. "Hey."

"What is it?"

He reached forward and removed something from her shoulder. A blowsy, overblown, gorgeously fragrant magnolia flower. He held it out to her, tucking it behind her ear.

For a second, his expression was intense as he gazed at her; he seemed almost a stranger. Something about the way his gaze rested on her gave her a funny feeling in her chest.

Then he grinned, and her friend was back.

NICK CAVALLO sipped bourbon and resumed his place, lounging with his elbows on the verandah rail. Not all the bourbon or all the cigars in the world could dispel his frustration.

And it wasn't merely sexual frustration that boiled within him, but frustration at his own stupidity.

Genna must have seen them.

He cursed softly.

The irony of the situation wasn't lost on him. He indulged in casual relationships, such as the one he'd almost had tonight, because it wasn't fair to date women with commitment in mind. He was already committed. Had been for four years, ever since he fell completely, crazily and hopelessly in love with his fiancée's bridesmaid, Genna Monroe.

And—based on the shell-shocked look on her face—if she'd recognized him in the garden, that should just about blow any chance he might ever have with her straight to hell.

As far as he could tell, she was a corporate version of Sleeping Beauty, so wrapped up in work she'd crammed her sexuality into a coma. For four long years he'd waited, learning her so well that when a prince handy with his lips was needed, he'd know it— and be right there to deliver the goods.

As seduction plans went, he had to admit it had a few flaws, but Nick was short on options. He blew out more smoke, then stubbed out the cigar in disgust.

Were Genna's blue eyes blind? He'd cancelled his wedding because of her, lobbied his brains out getting her hired on at the firm where he worked. His "reward" was the torment of spending the bulk of his week with her while she treated him like her goddamn brother.

He'd been so close to asking her out after he and Marcy broke up. The three of them were sitting around together when Marcy had laughingly said that he and Genna had so much more in common than he and Marcy did—a fact he'd certainly noticed—they should go out together.

Marcy had already found Darren by then. The man she'd end up marrying—the right man for her. Suddenly she was into matchmaking.

He'd never hit a woman in his life, never wanted to until that moment, but he could cheerfully have slugged his ex-fiancée for her giggling tactlessness. Before he could say a word, Genna had laughed. "Way too much in common. We'd drive each other crazy. No. Nick's like the big brother I never had."

He didn't want to be her damn brother. He wanted to be her lover. One day she'd see the light. In the meantime, he kept his sexual relationships commitment-free. Not usually as brief as tonight's, but he wasn't a man to turn down a beautiful woman when she offered herself. He wasn't going to be a monk, not even for Genna.

He wasn't going to hang around a balcony mooning over her like some ridiculous Romeo, either. He spared a glance to the reception and shuddered. Instead, he headed swiftly out of the hotel.

Suddenly, he craved the slow sobbing wail of a sax, the moody tempo of a lovelorn crooner. If he couldn't have Genna in New Orleans he could for damn sure have some blood-stirring jazz.

I WANT YOU. I want to be deep inside you when you come.

With a gasp, Genna sat up, cotton nightie sticking to her skin, heart pounding. Restless, she threw back the covers and opened the doors to the lacy wrought-iron balcony. So charming, so Creole, so blasted romantic.

Her room overlooked the walled garden where, only a few hours ago, she'd overheard the stranger. Since then, his seductive voice had entered her ear like some kind of twisted love potion and played havoc with her brain.

"What's the matter with me?" she asked the moon.

She wasn't a dedicated moon watcher, but here she couldn't seem to help gazing at the full golden orb that dominated the night sky, heavy and voluptuous. No wonder she couldn't stop thinking about sex. Even the damn moon was sexy.

Drawing the drapes with a jerk, she poured herself a glass of water and drank thirstily.

This was just plain crazy. Men were fine. She liked them. One day she planned to marry one. But right now her life was about work. She wanted that partnership so badly she could taste it, and she worked brutal hours, sacrificed a personal life so she could have it. Then, when she made partner, she could think about the next step on her life plan.

Looking for a mate.

But not yet. She had no room in her life for a man, and she certainly didn't have time for some bizarre obsession with a stranger.

Having sorted that out to her satisfaction, she got back into bed, shut her eyes firmly, and at last fell asleep once more.

You're so wet. Are you wet for me?

She moaned, reaching for him, and woke to find her arms empty, the faint scent of magnolia perfuming the air.

With a start, she sat up once again and flicked on the bedside lamp. The pool of lamplight illuminated the blossom she'd placed in a water glass. The one Nick had pulled off her shoulder earlier that night— the one that had fallen from the tree while it was shaken by passion.

Just as she'd been shaken.

She stared at it a moment, the pale blossom so innocent, the scent so potent and evocative. She reached a hand out to touch one creamy petal, and sighed. She ought to throw the thing away. But she knew she wouldn't.

She also knew she wouldn't sleep any more tonight. Giving in to the inevitable, she got out of bed, settled herself at the desk, then flipped on her laptop and checked her e-mail. This weekend retreat was supposed to be work-free, but she'd hiked a caseful with her, and now she was glad. While she made notes and researched recent incidents of sexual harassment, she could forget that mesmerizing voice.

Or she could try.

The CEO claimed sexual harassment had affected her work. Genna began noting specific occurrences.

Are you wet for me? She gasped and shook her head. She, Genna, was feeling harassed by her own memories.

They were definitely sexual. They were most certainly interfering with her work. She should sue that stranger. Or maybe her case was really against herself.

By six o'clock she felt the pangs of caffeine withdrawal. She double-checked the exact time on her watch then showered quickly, toweled her short blond

hair, dressed in white cotton slacks and a sleeveless
turquoise cotton sweater, then slipped on sandals.

As she dabbed on lip gloss with one hand, she
grabbed her bag and laptop in the other. She glanced
at her watch as she opened the door and nodded in
satisfaction. It had taken her fourteen minutes from
the moment she stepped into the shower to the moment she left her room. Wasting time was like wasting money, and Genna didn't believe in doing either.

She set off to find something to eat and a newspaper, smugly pleased with herself for putting in half
a day's work before seven.

Even at this early hour the lobby wasn't deserted.
A desk clerk yawned, cleaning staff polished a section
of marble tile, and a pair of muscular legs strode into
her line of vision. She raised her gaze and took in
black running shorts, a T-shirt that shouted at her to
Just do it, and Nick's unshaven face, his eyes heavy-
lidded, his short black hair tousled.

"Let me guess, you're briefing a client," she
teased. One of the many things they had in common
was a love of early mornings.

He shook his head. "Case in court."

She chuckled.

"If you want to come along, I'll wait while you
change."

It was tempting. They did run together sometimes,
although he had to slow his pace so she didn't have
a coronary by mile two. She knew she could up her
physical stamina, but she didn't have time to devote
to more regular fitness. Maybe after she made partner.

Right now, the thought of rich, black coffee was a
whole lot more enticing than huffing and puffing in

Nick's wake. "I need coffee more than exercise. Why don't you meet me at that little café we passed yesterday in the French Quarter?"

"The one with the parrot?"

"Mmm-hmm."

"I'll be about an hour."

"Fine. I'll just be reading the paper."

He gestured to the laptop she'd tried to conceal behind her. "Not working at all?"

She feigned innocence. "Oh, this? I just need my Free Cell fix."

He shook his head at her, but at least she didn't get another lecture on being a workaholic. "Liar. I'll walk you out."

On the sidewalk they parted. He turned toward the river and she crossed Canal Street to head into the Quarter. The morning was already warming as she strolled along, stepping around a small construction crew replacing the roof of a two-hundred-year-old town house.

She loved the architecture, with its mixture of Spanish, French and American styles, the shutters, the balconies, the rich colors of freshly painted plaster and the sun-bleached pastels. The bumpy sidewalks dotted with round metal disks one café owner had told her were termite traps. They added to the sense she had in this city that it was a lot of work to keep up appearances. The grandeur of the past wasn't just fading, it was being chewed up by insects.

On Bourbon Street she stepped around a broken string of purple Mardi Gras beads and an empty take-out cup. The smell of spilled booze and disinfectant mingled. Up ahead a shopkeeper hosed the sidewalk in front of a souvenir shop. Here, in party city, the day started slowly as though it was always the morning after.

She found the café and chose a spot where Nick could see her from the street. Then, over a coffee and a beignet, she tried to read the paper and forget about last night. Having whiled away half an hour, she got a second cup of coffee and, after a hasty glance up and down the street, flipped on her laptop.

Even as she pored over her notes on the sexual harassment case, she found her concentration wandering. Which never happened. Single-minded, focused, disciplined—these were the terms people used to describe her. Words she would use to describe herself. But each time she turned her attention to the words on the screen, a whisper pulled her back into a moonlit, scented garden.

She dropped her head into her hand and closed her eyes. How could a sexual encounter that hadn't even been hers have affected her so? Maybe she was losing her mind.

"Genna? Are you all right?" Once more, a male voice interrupted her thoughts, but this one was loud and clear, recognizable and very welcome.

She raised her head and forced a smile. "I'm fine, just tired. How was your run?"

"Great." Nick looked damp, but good. Healthy and rested, unlike her strung-out self. He gestured to her empty cup. "Want another?"

She hesitated a moment, but what difference would a third cup of coffee make? Her nerves were already jittery, and that had nothing to do with caffeine.

He returned with a huge bottle of water tucked under his arm and two steaming cups. After downing half the water, he took a sip of coffee and sighed with deep contentment. A man at peace with himself and his world. How she envied him.

She jiggled the spoon around in her cup, wondering if she needed a psychiatrist.

"What's on your mind, Gen?"

Startled, she glanced up to see serious gray eyes completely focused on her. "I'm just tired." She dropped her gaze. "I didn't sleep well."

"We've been friends a long time. If there's something bothering you..."

He was right. They were good friends. But still, he was a guy. Could he possibly understand what she was going through? She exhaled noisily. What the hell. If she went stark, raving bonkers he'd find out soon enough. "I think I'm losing my mind."

The gray eyes crinkled at the corners. "Do you want a second opinion on that?"

"Something happened last night...I—" She felt herself begin to blush. "Never mind. I can't explain it to you."

"Try." His voice sounded serious, urgent even.

"I think I need a psychiatrist."

"I took psychology 101 at college. I think I even got an A."

She bit her lip and gazed at him. "You'd have to promise not to tell a soul."

"Give me a dollar."

"What?"

"Give me a dollar and you've retained me as counsel. Attorney-client privilege. I can't tell anyone."

"I don't need a lawyer," she said, wishing she hadn't brought up the subject.

"Maybe not, but I think you need the counsel part."

He was right. So, she kept her eyes on her cup and told him. "I went for a walk in the garden behind our hotel last night. I...accidentally overheard a couple.... They were...making love."

"Did you see them?" His voice sounded odd, as if he'd scorched his throat on his coffee.

"No. I was behind a thick bush. I only heard them." She glanced up, not wanting him to think she was some kind of pervert. "I would have left as soon as I realized what they were doing, but I couldn't get by without them seeing me, so I decided to wait it out."

"So you feel like a voyeur? Is that it?"

"No. No. It's not that. It's the man..."

"What about the man?" he prompted, leaning closer.

"God, this is the insane part. It's so hard to explain. It was his voice." She stared into coffee as dark and rich as the garden last night. She grew warm just thinking about what had occurred. "He was whispering to the woman. Saying things... Wonderful, erotic things..."

"And?"

She gulped. "And I wanted him. I wanted him to do those things to *me*. I just sat there on this cold stone bench getting...turned on. He was probably as close to me as you are now, so close it could have been me he was whispering to. I...I— Oh, God." She dropped her head in her hands once more.

"You fantasized about making love with a stranger. Lots of women do. It's normal."

She risked a glance at him, but he didn't seem repulsed by her confession. He had a half smile on his face.

"Really?"

He shrugged. "That's what they told me in psych 101."

She grinned in spite of herself. Somehow this wasn't as bad as she'd thought it would be. She even felt bold enough to keep her gaze on his face as she confessed the worst part. "The thing is, I can't stop thinking about him, about his voice. Nick, I want him. I don't have a clue who this man is, but I want him so badly I can't sleep. I can't even concentrate on work."

He tapped his fingers on the metal tabletop. "Are you sure you want him?"

A frown drew her brows together. "I just told you I can't stop thinking about him."

"But is it the man or the fantasy you really want? What if you find out the guy's the hotel janitor? A sixty-year-old fat bald guy who's married? Hell, for all you know it could be me."

She laughed. "It couldn't be you. If you and I were going to be attracted to each other, it would have happened by now, wouldn't it?"

He shrugged, then picked up his water bottle and drank deeply.

She watched the muscles in his neck working, noticed a lazy droplet of sweat trickle its way down toward his T-shirt. "You're right, though, it could be anybody. That's what makes it so insane."

He wiped his mouth with the back of his hand and put the cap back on the water bottle. "I don't think you're insane. I think you've been working too hard. You're a young woman with a whole load of needs that aren't being met. Maybe you need to loosen up a little and start having some fun."

"I won't make partner if I don't put in the hours. Last year I billed two thousand hours. This year I hope to beat that. I don't have time for a personal life."

"So, when are you going to get one?"

"Get what?"

"A life."

"You mean sex?"

He shrugged. "If you want to put it that way."

"After I make partner. Then I'll look for a life partner."

He hadn't looked disgusted when she'd confessed her obsession with a stranger, but now his expression turned faintly contemptuous. "You've got it all mapped out, haven't you?"

"Don't make fun of me. You're just as driven as I am. I've seen the women you date, they're all impossible. They never last long because you choose women who won't commit."

Nick leaned back in his chair and shoved a stray lock of damp black hair off his forehead. "Looks like I'm not the only one who took psych 101."

"Sorry. That was out of line."

"Yes. Also correct. I date those women for a reason."

"Which is?"

He gazed at her for a long moment. "Someday, I

may just tell you. But now, we should get back. The sessions start in an hour.'' He stood.

She wrinkled her nose at him. ''And you need a shower.''

As they strolled back toward the hotel, he asked, ''What are you wearing tonight?''

''Tonight? Oh, the Mardi Gras thing. I rented a mermaid costume. How about you?''

''A shark.''

She chuckled. ''Very appropriate for a lawyers' do.''

2

GENNA STRAIGHTENED her tail fins as she entered the hotel ballroom, feeling as out of place as a real mermaid would. She'd liked the costume fine when she spotted it in the rental shop. It wasn't too revealing—the bodice was cut high and the sequined fabric covered most of her body—and the thing fit, so she'd taken it. Now the costume felt kind of...shiny.

A room hostess threw a handful of Mardi Gras beads over her head, green and gold and purple. Just what she needed, more glitz.

She glanced around, and was reassured to see sparkle, glitz and glamour everywhere. Almost a third of the lawyers at Donne, Green and Raddison were women. Some of the senior support staff—most of whom were female—had also been invited on the retreat, so the gender balance wasn't as bad as she'd feared. The organizers had even included a five-piece band with a sultry crooner for those who wanted to dance.

Even though they were weeks past the real Mardi Gras, everybody had made an effort to dress up. Royalty from every major country and era was represented, as was most of Greek and Roman mythology. It made for some interesting sights. Bacchus, drinking from a glass so large Genna suspected it was a flower vase, seemed well suited to his part if not his place in history. He was ogling Marie Antoinette.

She counted two Scarlett O'Haras and several Rhett Butlers, while Little Bo Peep seemed to have forgotten all about her sheep while in deep conversation with a shark.

Ah, a shark. Between the masks, the conversations and the fact that many of the staff in the three-hundred person firm were strangers to her, she didn't immediately recognize many people. It was a good thing Nick had mentioned his costume.

She made her way toward the shark and Bo Peep, pausing to chat for a moment with Nero, who sounded a lot like the managing partner. While she traded pleasantries, a waitress offered a tray. "Mint juleps? Or can I get you folks something else?"

"When in Rome, eh?" Nero smirked. He took two drinks off the tray and passed Genna one.

"Thanks." She'd already discovered that the mint part of the famous drink was a couple of green leaves floating on the top. The julep was, as far as she could tell, straight bourbon.

She made her way to join Little Bo Peep and the shark, who weren't talking about missing livestock but about a company buyout. The shark nodded briefly at Genna and said, "The thing is, Gwen, if company A buys company B for stock instead of cash, knowing it's not going to hit its quarterly earning forecast, which will for damn sure mean a big drop in the stock price, then company B could sue company A. You want to be careful on that one."

Since when had Nick turned into such a bore?

Come to think of it, his voice didn't sound right, either. "Nick?"

The shark shook his massive black head. "Harry Bentley. Mergers and Acquisitions." He eyed her costume. "Fellow sea creature. Have we met? Hard to tell with these masks. This is Gwen Davies, also from M and A."

"I'm Genna Monroe, in litigation. Nice to meet you both. I thought you were someone else. Don't let me interrupt." And she moved away while they returned to their takeover discussion.

Gazing around, she noticed a couple more sharks. Nick's costume hadn't been as original as she'd thought. She sipped the drink in her hand and found, now that her tongue was basically numbed by alcohol, that it wasn't that bad; the fiery taste seemed to match the wild jazzy beat of the band.

She should mingle. This might look like a party, but lots of lawyers would be talking business, like Harry and Gwen.

Her blood picked up the beat of the band and her eyes strayed to the dance floor. For a few moments she stood watching the swaying couples, barely aware that her own body was swaying in time to the music.

"Would you like to dance?" a voice whispered in her ear. No. Not *a* voice. *The* voice.

His voice.

It couldn't be, and yet, amazingly, unbelievably, the exotic whisperer was here at a dress-up party. She'd already reasoned that the man in the garden might well be with her firm, but hadn't dreamed she might meet him. She turned, nerves strung taut, to see the man who'd haunted her dreams, both sleeping and waking, for two days.

And in spite of everything she'd told herself, he wasn't a disappointment in the flesh. He was magnificent.

It was Neptune. From the gold crown on his head to his trident, the man was the king of the oceans. His broad chest suited the old-fashioned breastplate. He was tall, definitely not bald, and even though his face was covered in a gold mask, she got the impression of youth and power.

Her pounding heart was louder than the drums, her breath caught in her throat as she tried to inhale. "Who are you?" she finally managed to croak.

"Neptune. I rule your kingdom, so you must do anything I ask." Still, he whispered, and once again that voice sent secret desires chasing each other inside her.

"Who—who are you really?" Her heart banged so loudly against her ribs she barely heard her own words.

He touched her chin, let his finger travel down her throat and she almost gasped at the way his touch burned. "You know who I am. I saw you. In the garden."

Even though she'd known it was him, his calm reminder made her pulse jump and her face warm beneath her sequined half mask. "You knew I was there?"

"Not until…after. I saw you."

"I wasn't— I mean I didn't mean to eavesdrop. I just couldn't—"

"I know." His whisper understood, soothed.

"That woman. Is she here?"

He shook his head, his crown catching the light from an overhead crystal chandelier so it looked as if it were shooting sparks of fire. "She's gone. There was nothing between us. It meant nothing."

She nodded.

"It is you I want. Tonight."

Ooh. She was melting for him already, wanting him, needing him. Twenty-eight years of rigid control, of self-discipline and focus, and she was turning to jelly for an incognito hunk in a plastic crown and goofy mask. *Have we been working too hard, Genna? Yes, indeedy.* But, for the moment, she really didn't care.

It was glorious to be completely, selfishly, in lust with a total stranger. One who didn't know her LSAT scores, who didn't care that she could name all the presidents, including their terms of office, in order, forwards or backwards. Who didn't give a damn that she was the reigning office queen of casebook law.

He was probably a co-worker. With an internal giggle of glee she realized she didn't give a hoot.

Taking her silence for acquiescence, he commandeered her elbow in a delightfully chauvinistic way and steered her toward the dance floor. A sudden thought made her pause and glance up at him. She might be reckless, but she had standards. "Are you married?"

"No." Now she thought about it, he'd asked the Spanish woman that same question, so he was probably telling the truth.

She held his gaze for a second, what she could see of it. His mask was cut so that very little was visible.

A gleaming darkness shone through slits the size of dimes. Were his eyes round or almond? Impossible to tell. Hazel? Gray? Brown? Deep blue? Again, impossible to be certain.

Ditto with his marital status, come to that. Narrowing her own gaze, she grabbed his green-leather gloved left hand but discovered no wedding-ring-shaped lump. Either he didn't wear a ring, or he really wasn't married.

"Trust me, I'm single."

"I'm a lawyer. I trust nothing." Still, it was just a dance. She had time to decide if she wanted anything more from Neptune and his trident.

Something bluesy and very New Orleans was playing when he pulled her into his arms. Long, wailing sax notes, interspersed with a woman's voice singing an old love song as the stranger pulled her body flush against his.

He felt so warm, so solid, so…right. He was a perfect fit, his shoulder at just the height to lay her head on. She drank in his scent greedily: leather from his costume, soap, the hotel's shampoo and healthy adult male.

"I knew we'd dance well together," he whispered.

"Mmm."

They drifted, as at home in the music as if they really were floating undersea. She let her eyes drift shut and gave her overtired brain permission to have the night off. She wasn't relaxed. She'd probably never been less relaxed, but it was a kind of tension that made her body feel so heavy she needed to lean against Neptune, knowing he'd support her.

"I want to make love to you."

Even though she'd been obsessing about hearing this man say those words to her, she still felt the shock of them along her nerves. She deflected them with sarcasm, needing a little breathing room. "That's quite the line you have. Does it always work?"

"I'm serious. I want you, just as I know you want me."

"Mmm." She raised her head and forced her eyes open. "I didn't mean that as a yes."

"Didn't you?"

"I meant it like, you're a very attractive man and… Uh…could one mint julep have made me intoxicated?"

"You're not drunk. Just relaxed."

"You sound surprised."

She felt the muscles of his shoulders tense and relax under her cheek as he gave a small shrug. "I get the impression you're a pretty tense person most of the time."

"Not with you. You're a stranger. I can be anyone, do anything." She smiled secretly into his shoulder. "That's very liberating."

He ran his hand down her back and she started to melt. Slipping one hand beneath her hair, he held the back of her head and brought his lips slowly to hers. It took about seven years for his lips to reach her, and she enjoyed every tingling, tense second of anticipation. At last they met, like two old friends, like two new lovers, and she sighed with the pleasure of it.

Somehow, her fantasy seemed to be coming true. Quite possibly, she really had lost her mind and was fantasizing this whole thing. But, just for now, it didn't matter. When her lips began to tremble with the wanting, he licked around the edges before taking possession of her mouth.

Her closed eyelids kept out the garish light. Noise ebbed away. There was nothing in the world but this kiss. She'd waited her whole life for it. She clung to his lips and welcomed his tongue, invading, ravaging, inciting her. She felt the edges of the mask press against her skin and for a second recognized how unlike herself she was acting. This wasn't Genna Monroe, kissing a stranger at a company party. This was some wild, exotic creature who'd been hiding inside. And she wasn't hiding anymore.

The wild woman wanted this man and she wanted him now. She dragged her lips away from his and panted. "Ask me. Ask me now."

"I'm not asking." His whisper was part growl. "I'm taking what's mine." He grabbed her hand and strode toward the nearest door.

"Where are we going?" Not the garden. If they were interrupted, she'd die.

"My room."

His room gave him too much control. "My room."

He didn't quibble. "Lead the way."

Color and sparkle blurred as they made their rapid way through the ballroom. It was quieter once they got to the elevator, and Genna felt foolish as a couple of tourists stared at them. But, once the elevator doors closed, they were alone again. They lunged for each other with greedy passion, barely grabbing a breath as they rose twenty-two floors.

Once on her floor, she had a moment's unease. She halted in the middle of the corridor wondering what on earth she was doing. She turned to the man at her side, but as she opened her mouth to speak, he brought his down in a kiss that left her no room for conscious thought.

It was as though all the sexuality she'd kept bottled up had burst through her reserve like molten lava through the earth's crust. As hard as she might try, she couldn't force it back down. So, she went with the flow, never breaking contact until they got to her door. She fumbled the key card so badly, he took it from her and opened the door.

"Will you trust me?" he whispered.

She'd already made that decision or she wouldn't be alone with him in her hotel room. "Yes."

He walked across the room. She watched him, his form silhouetted against the moonlit window. Then those powerful arms drew the curtains, plunging the room into utter darkness.

A deep, gentle trembling began in her belly and spread outward.

She knew why she trembled. She had some control over the fantasies that stayed safely inside her head, but now one had become flesh....

Here, in this room, the king of the deep held sway.

Even as she tried to orient herself in the darkness, tried to work out just where the door was, she heard his voice, inches from her ear. "I've taken off my mask. Do you want the light?"

Did she? In the light he might be just as ordinary as Harry Bentley, and she no more than another merger, or acquisition, depending on how he looked on these things. He might make demands on her time, her attention, her emotions. No. Apart from being the most erotic thing she'd ever done, this was also time-efficient. By the very nature of its anonymity, this rendezvous would last no longer than one night.

"No. I like it dark," she said. "I know you're not married, but is there any reason we shouldn't do this? I mean, could there be embarrassment or repercussions for either of us?"

"Hush."

"I just think—"

"Don't think. Feel. Let me make you feel things you've never felt before."

Oh, it was so tempting to let go, to give her career-track mind a break, and let her deeper fantasies take over. But she couldn't let go before taking care of one important issue. "Did you bring condoms?"

"Yes."

She licked her lips nervously, wishing he'd touch her again. "It's nice to know the sea god comes prepared."

"Do you know what I want?"

He wanted to make love to her, slow, glorious, worshipful love. He had told her so but she wanted to hear him say it again.

"No. Tell me what you want." Because he whispered, so did she, and it was a husky sound she didn't think she'd ever made before in her life.

"I want you to strip off all your clothes, as if you were doing a striptease for an audience."

"But it's dark. You won't be able to see a thing."

"You'll have to describe it to me."

How did he do this to her? No sooner did he make the suggestion than her flesh began to tingle with warmth. A striptease in the dark was just about the silliest thing she'd ever heard, so why did it feel so wickedly sexy? She couldn't help the little smile that played round her mouth as she said, "All right. Turn your back until I'm ready."

A quiet chuckle answered her.

"No peeking." She took a deep breath, closed her eyes, imagined a smoky strip club, men's eager eyes on her, imagined herself strutting in high heels down the stage, confident and bold. "I'm ready."

She heard the shifting of bed springs and knew he'd settled on the king-size bed to "watch." "I can't identify the song. What's playing?"

"'You Can Keep Your Hat On.' Joe Cocker." And just like that she heard the unmistakable bump and grind and the sexy, stripper lyrics playing in her head. She began to move, strutting and dancing to the music. She was free, wild, exotic. The Mardi Gras beads began to clack and clatter like quiet applause.

"What are you taking off first?"

"My tail fins."

"Good call."

She kept her rhythm going while she fiddled with the velcro tabs and zipper that finally released her from her mermaid's tail. She tossed it aside and it hit the floor like manic castanets.

"Now what are you wearing?" If a whisper could get huskier, his just had.

"A very pretty blue-green cloth mask, a sequin-and-net bodice, panties—" Damn, she also wore panty hose. No way she was ruining her mental image—or this sexy stranger's—with panty hose. She slipped them off as quietly as she could. "High heels, a few beads and a smile." She stepped back into her heels as quickly and quietly as she could as she divested herself of the nylons and chucked them to another corner.

"What color panties?"

She swallowed, as her body began to feel heavy and liquid. She could barely get the word out. "Black."

"Come here."

Trying to sound like a bored stripper, she said, "Sorry, sir, you're not allowed to touch, only look."

"But I've got a crisp twenty dollar bill to tuck into those black panties."

"Oh." She gulped, feeling like she was already getting out of her depth in the sexual game-playing department. Besides, he probably thought they were sexy silk bikinis, not black cotton sports briefs.

She heard the crackle of a bill and knew he was taunting her. Fine. She gyrated her way to the foot of the bed, where a darkness loomed like a solid shadow. Warmth radiated from him as she approached.

Even though she'd expected it, his touch on her belly made her suck in her breath. He traced a finger from her right hip to her navel, leaving a trail of goose bumps in his wake, then slipped his hand lower, under the waistband of her panties. She quivered as his fingers just brushed her curls. Then she felt the papery stiffness of the bill scrape her flesh lightly as he tucked it in and removed his hand. "I like your style of dancing."

"Thank you, sir."

She backed off a few steps, the music playing louder in her head. She was seriously getting into this, feeling the utter concentration of her audience, the erotic temperature rising swiftly in the room. She could have sworn she heard ice clink in glasses, and smelled cigarette smoke, felt the stage beneath her feet. "I hope you're paying attention, sir. I'm taking off my top now."

"Oh, honey. You've got my attention."

She unzipped the side zipper with a slow hiss, and just for fun, danced around a bit with the top held against her breasts, teasing him even though he couldn't see. She'd never had so much fun, or felt more seductive in her life. "Are you ready for my naked breasts?" she taunted.

"Oh, yeah."

She tossed the bodice across the room to join the rest of her costume. Now she wore nothing but panties, heels and her mask, but he didn't know that. "I'm going to swing my gold tassels now. Don't get dizzy."

"I already am."

She'd seen a stripper once, in college, and the woman had had amazing muscle control, she now realized, as she tried to mimic those seductive moves. It didn't feel like her breasts were making circles as she jiggled and swung her shoulders and torso. It felt more like trying to juggle chunks of Jell-O. Still, in her mind's eye, those tassels were twirling like propellers.

The ache inside her was growing. She wanted to touch Neptune, have him touch her.

Her hips were gyrating, her head swinging to the same rhythm. The friction of her panties against her body was driving her wild. She worked her way around in a circle just in front of him. "I'm going to take off my panties now."

"How much for them?"

She was so surprised she forgot to play her role. She stopped dead, the music in her head silenced. "Huh?"

"For your panties. How much?"

Did strippers do this kind of thing? She had no idea, but she respected an exotic dancer's right to make an honest profit. "Fifty bucks."

"I'll give you a hundred if you let me take them off."

A little whimper caught in her throat. She was so hot, she was surprised her panties didn't combust. "All right." Once again she moved to stand in front of him.

He touched her then. Just a finger tracing the elastic waistband. When he got to the twenty he'd tucked in earlier, he removed it and she felt him shift as he leaned over to toss the money on her night table.

He eased the cotton panties down her legs, dropping to his knees in front of her, and, from feeling like a wanton stripper, something about the reverence in his movements made her feel like a brand-new bride.

He put a hand behind her knee and lifted, raising her foot. He pulled the panties over her shoe, then removed the shoe letting it fall to the carpet. He repeated the process with the other leg.

Now she was naked but for her mask.

"You're beautiful." His words puffed warm breath onto her upper thigh.

"You can't see me."

"I can feel you." And he did. Running his fingers up her sides, he rose, and slid his hands over her shoulders before trailing them slowly and seductively down to her breasts. She sucked in a breath as big warm hands closed over her sensitive flesh, and he took advantage of her parted lips to kiss her deeply.

With a little sigh, she stepped closer, wrapping her arms around him. As she did, she gasped in shock at the impact of warm, bare flesh on warm, bare flesh. "You're naked!"

A soft chuckle rumbled against her lips. "I was hoping you'd notice."

"But I wanted *you* to strip for *me*."

"Maybe next time."

They both knew there'd be no next time, but she played along with the idea. "I'll make you strip under a spotlight. In a room full of women."

Then he snugged her body up tight to his and she felt his erection, gloriously heavy against her belly. Oh, how she wanted this.

Bending, he lifted her into his arms. She felt the warm roughness of a hairy chest against her side as he carried her to the bed and laid her gently down. Dimly, she realized he'd turned down the bed as well as stripped while she'd been dancing.

She heard the telltale rip of a condom package, and in a moment, he joined her in the bed. Reaching behind her, he untied her mask and tossed it aside.

She felt wonderfully free with this stranger. She could be and do anything, for this one crazy night. There was no hurry, and yet there was a curious urgency within her to experience everything with this man, to have her fill of him and give generously of herself.

If she gorged on him all night surely she'd get over her obsession.

Of course, she'd tried once to cure herself of a weakness for chocolate by binging on the stuff until the very sight of it made her feel ill. But it hadn't been successful. After a few days, she still loved chocolate just as much as ever.

She hoped she'd have more success tonight.

He shifted against her, warm, long and muscular. She ran her hands over his back, his arms, his chest. He was athletic, his belly flat. Unusual in a lawyer, in her experience.

His lips cruised over her lips, cheekbones, her nose, chin and throat, learning her face by touch as a blind man would. Oh, those lips were warm and firm, eliciting flutters and trembles wherever they touched. From her throat he trailed a lazy wet path to her breasts, tasting and sampling his way to her tight, throbbing nipples. When he sucked one into his mouth, she cried out, arching up off the bed at the amazing sensations spiraling through her body.

She felt the corresponding tug between her legs and couldn't lie still. Her lower body tossed restlessly against the cotton sheets.

He took his time over her breasts, before moving down to drop kisses across her trembling belly. When his big warm hands took hold of her thighs and nudged them apart, she spread herself before him eagerly.

In the garden, he'd told the Spanish woman everything he was going to do. Tonight, with Genna, he was silent. As much as she loved his sexy whisper, she was glad it was different with her. Besides, in the dark, every touch was a surprise—every silent pause filled with the excitement of waiting for his next move. She discovered it was just as sexy to wait and wonder where next his lips and hands would touch as it was to be told ahead of time what was coming.

She waited now for him to plunge into her, and she ached deep inside with the waiting. She felt him move, quivered in anticipation of the hard thrust, and instead she felt the wet assault of his tongue on her most vulnerable and sensitive spot.

She cried out, her body bucking helplessly. It was too much; she couldn't bear so much exquisite excitement. "No, wait…" But it was already too late. He sucked on her and she flew apart into a thousand glittering pieces.

She was still floating dreamily, when she felt welcome hardness at the entrance to her body. It seemed to her he hesitated, as though waiting politely to be invited inside.

"Yes." She invited him in with Southern hospitality that would make her New Orleans hosts proud. "Please."

He didn't need any more encouragement, but surged into her, filling and stretching her until she felt she couldn't take any more. She clawed at his shoulders, fingers sliding against his sweat-slick flesh, gasping at the overwhelming heat pounding through her.

It had been so long since she'd held a man inside her body, it felt almost like the first time. She'd forgotten the sensations: the pull of stretched flesh, soft against hard, rough against smooth. She'd forgotten the amazing intimacy of being interconnected with another human being. Or had she ever felt this way before?

He stayed still, his hips resting against hers, and kissed her lips, whispering nonsense endearments into her ear, giving her time to adjust to him. When she relaxed and sighed, he moved, slowly at first then faster, harder.

The sounds coming from her throat were wild and primitive as she arched up to receive him even as he thrust down into her, again and again as they pushed each other to ecstasy. For an endless moment he held her, suspended on the edge of the precipice, then with a groan he plunged, taking her with him to the deepest part of the ocean where he ruled.

When their last gasps had settled, he rolled to the side, tucking her under his arm. Her cheek resting on his chest, Genna, who prided herself on her control, lost it completely and burst into noisy, sobbing tears.

"OH, MY GOD. I'm sorry. I've hurt you." Nick held the sobbing woman in his arms, cursing himself for a clumsy fool.

He knew Genna hadn't been with anyone for a long time. He should have taken it more slowly, let her get used to him. He'd just waited so long for her, and then been so intoxicated with the moment, he hadn't been as gentle as he should have.

"No," she sobbed. "It's not—" But her voice was lost as new sobs shook her slim shoulders.

Feeling panicky now—what if she was in real pain?—he considered flipping on the light to check for damage. But how the hell would he know what to look for? She needed a doctor, or another woman at least. "Do you want me to call someone?"

"No." She shook her head, hair rustling against his chin and swallowed a sob. "I'm fine. It was just so beautiful."

"I didn't mean to be brutal. Swear to God."

She hiccupped on a giggle. "Not *brutal,* I said it was *beautiful.*"

It took him a stunned minute to realize she was crying happy tears. He blew out a breath and relaxed against her, feeling the wet tickle of a tear travel down his chest. He kissed the top of her head, rubbed her back and let her cry.

He didn't feel like crying. He felt like doing some kind of war whoop and then getting started all over again. He hadn't even begun to explore all the things he wanted to do in bed with Genna. Although, when he came to think of it, just holding her, naked and trusting against him like this, was right up there.

"I'm getting you all wet," she sighed. "I don't know what's wrong with me, I never cry. I just...I never thought it could be like that," she said.

He felt his chest swell with pride. He'd given her something special. Maybe his pent-up longing had made it extraspecial, because he had to admit, she was right. He'd never known sex could be like that, either. "You ain't seen nothing yet," he promised. "Well, give me another minute, then we'll see."

She chuckled, drying her cheeks with her hands, then trailed her fingers over his chest in a swirling rhythm he found both soothing and amazingly sexy. She had small hands, but they were so capable.

He'd seen them comfort clients, fly over her keyboard, tap her knees in frustration—always under the boardroom table, so it was hard to spot. He'd watched them flick her hair behind her ears, straighten pages into nice neat piles, but he'd never seen them in any kind of caress.

He couldn't now, of course. He could only feel the softness of her fingertips followed by the dragging scrape of her nails. He knew what they looked like, too, those nails. They could be a template for a career woman's nails. Not too long, not too short, polished in that fancy way that made them all white and pearly.

He sighed with contentment. If they had a lifetime together he could lie for hours with her head on his shoulder, and her hands running over his naked torso.

"I've never done anything like this before," she said softly.

"Why not?"

She took a moment to consider the question, while her fingers continued foraging in his chest hair. "I guess I take life pretty seriously. I've never wasted a lot of time…fooling around."

It was hard to carry on much of a serious conversation when he'd confined himself to whispering. It concealed his identity, all right; it was also giving him a sore throat. However, maybe she'd listen to this stranger, when she'd never listen to her good buddy Nick. "Every life is a path you travel," he whispered. "Make sure your path is of your own making."

"Wow, that's profound. Did you make it up?"

He took her earlobe between his teeth and bit down lightly, just to show her he wasn't a philosophizing dullard all the time. "Think about it. Stop sometimes to smell the magnolias."

"Would tonight count as stopping to smell the magnolias?" Her voice was as teasingly sensuous as the scent she described.

"Oh, it would," he agreed. He ran his fingers down the side of her neck and felt her shiver. "Prepare to smell the magnolias again, feel the earth move, hear choirs of angels, see—"

She cut him off by kissing him with such enthusiasm he was the one who heard the angels start to harmonize. Then she raised her head. "I never knew you sea gods were such braggarts. We mermaids have a few tricks of our own, you know.''

He felt the bedclothes shift, the slide of flesh against flesh, and next thing he knew, she was straddling him, making him believe she did have some kind of magic trick. For, if possible, he was harder now than he had been the first time, and just as strainingly eager.

Those beautiful, small, capable hands were everywhere, touching, skimming, pausing here and there as she learned his body. Every touch was a caress—every caress fired his blood.

Still feeling he might have hurt her somehow with his previous lack of restraint, he forced himself to lie as still as humanly possible while the woman of his dreams tormented him. The sweet, wet entrance he wanted so badly to penetrate hovered over him, brushing up and down his length, as though by accident, while she licked his throat.

Even as he was raising his hips to give her a little nudge in the right direction, she was backing off, tracing her hands down his sides, scraping her teeth over his nipples. Did she know how she was affecting him? He was damned sure she did.

''Heartless witch,'' he panted.

''Egotistical sea god.''

She rose over him slowly, finally taking pity on him. ''Mermaids rule,'' she informed him as she lowered herself, easing him slowly into her body.

Then she started moving on him and his mind just plain shut down and gave itself over to the exquisite sensation. She set the pace, at first as slow and thorough as a jury deliberation.

He felt the change in tempo as she started losing control. Helpless little sounds escaped her throat and those alone almost drove him over the edge. Faster she rode him, her flesh slapping his as she plunged against him until her soft gasps turned to a sobbing cry and that tight wet sheath clenched and shuddered all around him.

Not even King Neptune himself could hold out against that kind of pressure. With a thankful groan, he let himself go....

GENNA WOKE SLOWLY, her eyes feeling as if they'd been nailed shut, and her lips perma-glued into a smug smile.

Magnolia, she smelled magnolia.

She stretched languorously, trying to recapture her dream—it had been such a wonderful dream. Then with a gasp, she forced her eyes open as memory came flooding back.

It hadn't been a dream.

She'd made love the entire night with a total stranger.

Yanking the sheet to her chin, she jerked her head from side to side scanning the pillows, but there was no sign of the mystery man who'd taken her to the moon and back. On the now-empty pillow beside her was a stem of magnolia.

She smiled at the fragrant blushing bloom as she might have smiled at a lover. Reaching for the flower, she held it under her nose and breathed. She knew that forever more the smell of magnolia would bring her right back to this moment.

Her sleepy smile went south when she turned to

squint at the clock on the bedside table. Not only had she overslept, but in front of the clock lay two fifty dollar bills and a twenty.

For a second, her hand tightened in outrage on the hapless flower. Did her Neptune knock-off think she was a hooker?

Then, with a gasp, she recalled the man "buying" her underwear for a hundred bucks—after he'd stuck a twenty in her waistband. She'd played along, but she'd assumed he was joking.

Leaping out of bed, she conducted a quick but thorough search. There was no sign of her panties. They were a department-store brand of lingerie, nothing special. The only value they could have to her mystery lover was as a souvenir.

She dropped her head in her hands and groaned, "With my luck, they'll turn up on the Internet." And yet, somehow she was certain they wouldn't. She couldn't have said why it was, but she trusted her anonymous midnight lover.

She hoped she was right and he'd just toss them in the trash now he'd had his fun. And as for the money, it would be a big help to the soup kitchen she'd passed yesterday.

She stepped into a steaming shower and let hot water pummel her muscles—some of which ached from not having been used in a while. Whoever he was, her mystery lover had given her a night she'd never forget. She'd been so free, so unrestrained— God, she'd blubbered all over him—and where that came from she had no idea. It had just been so perfect. The sex, the man, the city. It felt like the most perfect moment of her life, and knowing it could never happen again had made her cry.

Mmm. But not for long. Was he thinking about her this morning? Wondering about her identity just as she pondered his?

She turned the tap to cold and danced around the tub gasping until she felt well and truly awake and alert. Shivering, she grabbed one of the hotel's big white fluffy towels and wrapped herself in it. Then her head shot up, encountering her own out-of-focus reflection in the steamy mirror.

What if he found out who she was?

Duh. How hard could it be? He had her room number for heaven's sake, and her mask hadn't obliterated her appearance the way his had. For a woman who'd put her career before everything, she'd just potentially deep-sixed any hope she ever had of making partner. Depending on whom she'd slept with and how big his mouth and his ego were, she might have jeopardized her entire career.

On legs that felt wobbly, she sank to the toilet seat, clutching the towel around her as though it were her reputation.

Again, that sense which had no basis in anything but instinct told her she could trust him. She blew out a shaky breath. If she were very, very lucky, this was over. He'd had his fun, she'd had hers.

Now, they could get on with their lives. Her obsession was officially cured and she'd never, ever do anything so stupid again. She wouldn't obsess about him anymore. She wouldn't even think about him.

She rose and wiped off an oval of mirror. Ruthlessly, she dragged a comb through wet tangles.

Her eyes stared back at her, slightly out of focus in the steamy mirror, looking distinctly pleased with themselves. Would she ever meet him again? And if she did, would she even know? Would some secret woman's intuition, some sexual-satisfaction phero-mone, alert her? Would she gaze into a stranger's eyes one day, perhaps hear his voice, and know that he was the one?

"Aaagh!" With a strangled cry, she heaved the comb at the mirror. "Get over it!" she shouted at her reflection.

HER DESK PHONE buzzed and Genna automatically glanced at her watch, noting the interruption on her time sheet. "Genna Monroe."

She smiled into the receiver as she said her name, a trick that hid her irritation at being interrupted, so a client wouldn't hear it in her voice.

It wasn't a client. It was Nick. So the smile fell into a natural curve and stayed in place.

"I need your help in a divorce case," he said.

She groaned and the smile went south. "You know I hate—"

"Everybody hates divorce cases." She heard the exasperation in his tone. "I don't usually do them, but this is the daughter of a big client so we're stuck with it."

"And this is my problem because…?" How could he possibly not know she was so burdened with work she practically bench-pressed her briefcase.

"We're representing a woman falsely accused of adultery by her husband." The exasperation was gone and a teasing note entered his voice. "And you, as you are so fond of telling me, are a feminist," he said with relish.

She couldn't hide her chuckle at his blatant con-artist tricks. "Oh, you are such a weasel. You're not going to talk me into this, you know."

"I could remind you that I'm a partner and not used to being referred to as an egg-sucking varmint."

"Then you'd just be acting more like a weasel." She settled back in her chair and pictured Nick doing the same in his much-larger office down the hall. He'd have his jacket off, sleeves rolled up and tie loosened. He might glance out of his window and watch the traffic on the lake.

Her view was of the hallway and the secretary she shared with two other associates. A view that would change when she made partner, when she started delegating grunt work.

"I really need your help on this one," he said, "because you're the best."

Oh, yeah. He was pulling out all the stops. "I'm not falling for this, Nick."

She pictured his lazy grin as he tried to dump his unwanted case on her already burdened shoulders, knowing, as they both did, that she'd do the job and do it well. But she didn't have to be gracious about it, not with an old friend like Nick. And she didn't have to let him know that she'd look forward to working with him—even if it was a divorce case. They'd both been so busy they'd barely seen each other in the week they'd been back in Chicago.

His chuckle traveled over the phone line, rich and low. "It really might interest you. I'll tell you about it when we meet. Three o'clock suit you?"

Did he really think he was getting off that easily? He'd have to work harder than that. A little groveling might even be required. "And if I were to ease your burden by helping with this nuisance case, the bribe would be?"

A long-suffering sigh told her she had him where she wanted him. "Name your price."

She thought of dinner at Charlie Trotter's, courtside tickets to the Bulls, a gorgeous pair of shoes she coveted at Nieman Marcus, but she was a practical woman. "My kitchen faucet leaks."

"You want me to hire a plumber?" He sounded confused. He must have thought he'd get away with a nice dinner. *Gotcha!*

"I want *you* to fix the leak. You can let yourself into my condo anytime. You've got the key."

"I never should have told you my dad was a plumber," he grumbled. But she wasn't fooled. She knew he loved working with his hands and getting dirty. And she didn't have time to mess with the yellow pages and strangers in her home.

"Deal?"

"How bad's the leak? If it's really pouring out you should—"

"It's a slow drip and I have a bucket under the sink. The job can wait on your schedule."

"All right. I'll try to get to it this weekend. Deal. See you at three."

She was smiling as she noted she'd been on the phone for three minutes. Nick could simply have told her she'd be assisting him on the case. It was certainly his right. Instead he'd made it fun—and agreed to fix her leaky faucet.

He was such a good friend.

GENNA SLIPPED ON her suit jacket and headed to her three-o'clock meeting in Nick's office, trying not to frown.

As a child of divorced parents herself, she hated divorce cases. She hoped this couple didn't have kids.

As she strode down the carpeted hallway she thought about how much she liked being single. She didn't worry about *her* marriage ending in divorce, and she was free of other problems, as well.

She smiled automatically at the paralegal approaching her while her train of thought continued. No scheduling conflicts, no stupid arguments about whose turn it was to take out the garbage, no meals to prepare when she wasn't hungry, no smelly male gym socks on her bathroom floor. *No mind-altering sex.*

"You okay there, Genna?"

"Hmm? Oh, yes. Thanks. I just tripped on…" She stared at the smooth carpet ahead of her, marred by not so much as a fluffball. She'd tripped on her own thoughts, that's what. And her memories of one all-too-brief night. She mumbled something unintelligible, but by that time the paralegal had passed her.

A week had gone by since her glorious but ill-advised one-nighter. Instead of purging her obsession, the night of passion had merely intensified it.

She knew she'd never see him again. Ridiculous phrase. She hadn't seen him the first time. There'd only been sensation and shadows. Heat and desire melded into one. Where he touched her, ripples spread over her flesh, driving, heating her until her body began to ache.

She'd never again feel his strong body moving on her, in her, hear him whisper erotic suggestions in her ear, and she was terrified she'd never feel the passion in her own body she'd experienced in one night with a total stranger.

But Genna hadn't got as far as she had without tremendous self-discipline. She'd beat this craziness if it was the last thing she did.

Gripping her burgundy leather portfolio a little tighter, she strode down the hall, her thoughts all on business.

At the entrance to Nick's office, she heard him speaking, and tapped politely on the half-open door, in case the client should be within. She stuck her head into the office, but Nick was alone.

He gestured with his pen for her to enter, and made a face while he continued speaking into the phone. "Absolutely, Gerald. I feel for your daughter. A very awkward situation. I've got our top associate working closely with me on this one." He winked at her and she stuck her tongue out at him. "Absolutely. Highest priority." He rolled his eyes.

Genna grabbed a seat at the round conference table in his office, opened her portfolio, took out the gold ballpoint her dad had given her when she passed the bar, then noted the date and time of the meeting at the top of a clean white page.

"You're right, we haven't hit the fairways in a while. We'll have to do that soon," Nick agreed in a jovial, winding-down-the-conversation tone.

He wore a crisp white cotton shirt that didn't show a single crease. She'd be impressed with his domestic abilities if she didn't know he paid a fortune to have his shirts laundered.

She was just thinking about checking her e-mails

on her Palm Pilot when he finished the call. "Whew," he said, rising and snugging his tie closer to his neck. She noted how tanned his skin looked against the white of the shirt. Part of his Italian heritage no doubt, along with the slightly curly dark-brown hair.

The dark coloring only emphasized his clear gray eyes and added to his appeal. No wonder women were always falling all over him.

He unrolled his sleeves, covering strong forearms, and tried to button them. "That was dear old Dad on the phone. He wants the best for his daughter, and the best, apparently, is to make sure she comes out of this smelling like a rose."

She took pity on Nick's clumsy left-handed effort and crossed the room, taking his right wrist in her hands and efficiently buttoning the cuff.

"Damn, I hate divorces," he said.

"Is that why you've never married?" she asked, giving the cuff a tug to smooth out the wrinkles.

She glanced up to find his gaze resting on her, an odd expression in his eyes. "It's one reason," he said at last.

She took a step back and reached for the charcoal-gray suit jacket hanging on the back of his door. "Lousy case?" She stepped behind him and held out his jacket.

"Thanks." He slipped his arms in the sleeves. "They always are. Our client, Mrs. Ross, has a husband who accuses her of adultery. Which, according to Dad, never happened."

"Dads aren't always the most reliable witnesses. Adultery, huh? He's going for a fault divorce then?"

In Illinois, most divorces were no-fault. The two parties had to live apart for two years, claim irreconcil-
able differences and then divorce. However, it was
still possible to claim one party was at fault. Usually
because of adultery. It sped up the waiting period to
six months.

"Looks like it. Hubby's talking about trying to get
the kids."

Genna's heart sank. "Kids?"

"Three." The way he said the word she knew he
felt just as bad as she did that innocent children were
going to be dragged into this. She'd do everything
she could to make sure they didn't end up as pawns.

"Is he doing this because he's feeling angry and
vindictive? Or does he want to get married again in
a hurry?"

Nick shrugged. "I hope Mrs. Ross can help us with
that. Her dad's most worried about her trust fund."

She moved back to the conference table to note
these brief details. "So, what—" Nick's intercom
buzzed, his secretary informing him Mrs. Ross was
there.

"Thanks, Jan. Bring her right in."

Mrs. Ross was probably in her mid-thirties, with
curly black hair worn loose to her shoulders, a wide
mouth and an anxious expression in her brown eyes.
She wore a red suit and high heels, but from the way
she walked—as though each step hurt—Genna figured she didn't usually dress this way.

Nick gave the woman his most charming smile,
and, like most women, Mrs. Ross responded. Another
Italian trait he'd inherited from his ancestors. Exces-
sive charm.

He made the introductions and the three of them sat at the conference table. Genna was the only one making notes, but she was accustomed by now to the fact that Nick preferred to concentrate on the client. If he made notes, it would be after Mrs. Ross had left. And, of course, because Genna was more efficient than a court stenographer, she knew damn well he wouldn't have to bother.

After Mrs. Ross refused any refreshment, there was a tiny pause.

"I just got off the phone with your father, Mrs. Ross," Nick said. "He's very worried about you."

The woman's red lips trembled. "I know. This is just so…awful."

"Why don't you tell us the whole story."

"The story. Um…" She glanced at Genna, as though for inspiration. "I don't know where to start."

"Why don't you start with whatever happened that made your husband think you were unfaithful, Mrs. Ross," Genna suggested, her pen poised. *Cut to the chase*.

The woman's chin trembled and her hands clutched her purse. "Please, call me Tiffany."

"All right…Tiffany."

The woman opened her black leather handbag and Genna wondered if she was going for tissues. Although Nick—or his secretary—had thought ahead and there was a fresh box in the middle of the conference table.

It was a set of photographs that Tiffany emerged with after rummaging in the bag for a few seconds. Hastily she pulled the prints from the envelope and flicked through them, until she came to the one she wanted.

"This is when it all started." With a grimace, she shoved the picture across the table.

Genna had been in the law business long enough to see everything from dead bodies to sexual acts caught on film. She'd learned to show no reaction, no matter how violent or distasteful the image. In this case, all she felt was puzzlement.

The photo was a candid family shot. Mrs. Ross herself in a grubby-looking sweat suit, three kids, not one of whom looked old enough for school, and a heavyset man who appeared surprised to have stumbled into the picture.

She studied the photo, glanced at Nick, who gave an infinitesimal shrug, and turned back to their client. "I'm not sure I understand. Is that man...?"

"That's Rory, my husband."

Genna nodded understandingly, not understanding a damn thing and wishing she'd called a plumber to fix her faucet and told Nick to take a flying leap when he'd manipulated her into this.

Tiffany Ross picked up the picture as though it were radioactive and glared at it. Then, still staring at the photo as though she could not believe her eyes, she began speaking rapidly. "Don't you see? This is my life."

She glanced up first at Nick, then at Genna, an expression of horror on her face. "My life! I'm only thirty-six years old, and all I do is change diapers and clean house. A big day out is grocery shopping. My husband's hardly ever home and when he is he just watches TV. I love my kids, but I need more in my life. I need a man. But does Rory even try to help around the house? Does he ever change a diaper? Does he so much as kiss me when he gets home? I wouldn't even care if he'd just *talk* to me once in a while."

In the face of this woman's pain, Genna felt small experiencing the smug certainty that she'd been smart to avoid men and matrimony.

"Have you talked to your husband about your concerns?" Nick asked, a sympathetic frown creasing his forehead. Nick wouldn't be that kind of husband or father, Genna felt certain. She could see him with a baseball glove in hand, playing catch with a younger version of himself. A boy with curly brown hair and big gray eyes, and the image made her smile before she pulled herself back to listen to Mrs. Ross.

"Rory never listens to me, he just tells me I whine all the time. He says I'm no fun anymore. I'm no fun. How am I supposed to be fun when he never wants to do anything with me? So then we fight, and he goes out."

Now that she was rolling, the woman's eyes filled with tears. Genna pushed the tissues closer. "So you felt abandoned by your husband."

Tiffany nodded, sniffed and grabbed a tissue. "It's not like I don't love my family. I do. But I was just shriveling up inside. I guess I just stopped bothering. I never put on makeup or nice clothes—what's the point? We hardly ever even had sex." She sniffed again.

"And that was unusual?" Nick asked.

Their client nodded. "We used to do it all the time. And then one day I looked at the calendar and figured it had been a whole month. I thought Rory was having an affair.''

"Do you have any proof?'' Nick asked.

Tiffany just shook her head. "He says he never did. He says I'm just making excuses for what I did.''

Now, it seemed they were getting to the heart of the matter. Neither she nor Nick asked the obvious question. Now that she was off and running with her story, Tiffany would tell them in her own way.

The office was silent but for the sniffling noises Tiffany made as she wiped her eyes.

"One day, I was reading the paper. I like to read the personal ads. I don't know, I guess I like to imagine people out there finding each other. You know? Anyway, one day I saw this ad from a guy. And it was like he was talking to *me*.''

Genna pulled her gaze away from the window, getting a bad feeling in her stomach. "A personal ad.''

"Yes. I brought it with me.'' Once more she dug into her purse and this time she pulled out a torn page from a newspaper. She smoothed it out and pointed to one ad circled in purple crayon. Nick picked it up and read aloud.

"In the middle of your crazy hectic life, are you lonely?

"I am. A busy medical practice isn't enough to stop the loneliness I feel. I seek a warm and exciting woman for intimate conversation. You are a woman with experience of life, maybe a mother who cares about people. If you believe we could help each other please reply to box number...''

Nick put the scrap of newsprint back on the table and smoothed it. "Did you reply to the ad?" he asked, his voice, like his expression, neutral.

Tiffany bit her lip and nodded. "I kept it for a few days, not thinking I would. But Rory was out every single night that week and I just thought I'd go crazy if I didn't do something. I love Rory, I really do, but he just kept ignoring me. So finally I wrote to the guy."

"Did you keep a copy of your letter?"

She shook her head, staring at the ad on the table as if it had let her down somehow. "I remember what I said, though. I told him about myself and said I'd like to meet him for coffee. I'm not stupid. I wasn't going to give out my name or address, so I picked a coffee shop and told him what time I'd be there. I figured if he didn't show, it wasn't meant to be."

"He showed?"

She nodded, and a blush crept up her cheeks. "I said I'd meet him at 11:00 a.m. I can't describe what it was like." Again she looked at Genna, as though being another woman, she'd understand. Genna nodded encouragement, but in truth she couldn't imagine anything more foreign to her nature than to be duped by such an obvious ploy.

Tiffany's eyes sparkled at the memory, "It was like being in a movie, or a secret agent or something. I told him I'd wear black and carry a red rose."

"A red rose?" *Oh, puhlease.*

"Yes. I got there about a quarter of eleven. I ordered a cappuccino and sat at this table for two, watching the door. I remember my hands were shaking and my heart was pounding." Her hand crept to her chest to illustrate. "Just when I started thinking he wasn't going to show, this gorgeous young blond guy came running in the door with his hospital coat still on and a stethoscope sticking out of his pocket."

Genna began to think they were made for each other. Her with her red rose, and Doctor Phooey with his stethoscope. "Then what happened?"

"Well, he kind of glanced around and then he saw the rose, and he saw me, and it was like his whole face lit up. He came and sat down, but said he couldn't stay very long. He was in the middle of a difficult delivery, but he just had to come and meet me, my letter had meant so much to him. He even had it, in his pocket."

"With the stethoscope?" Genna asked before she could stop herself. Nick frowned at her.

But Tiffany was immune to the sarcasm; she was lost in her romantic fantasy. "Yes. It was kind of crumpled, as if he'd read it over and over."

"Did he give you his name?"

She sighed. It was as if she wasn't even in the room with them anymore. She was in the busy coffee shop, gazing adoringly at her pen pal. "Dr. Ersatz."

"Ersatz?" It was Nick who interrupted.

"That's right. Dr. Stephen Ersatz."

"Tiffany, do you know what *ersatz* means?"

She shrugged. "It's Polish, right?"

Nick and Genna exchanged glances. "No. It's not Polish. It's German. *Ersatz* means, well, it's something that pretends to be something else."

"Oh." Tiffany's face fell. "Well, I figured out later he wasn't a real doctor."

"How?" Genna figured he must have done something stupendously stupid if Tiffany had become suspicious.

"We were out once, in public, and he started making jokes about a patient's private parts." Tiffany's brown eyes sparkled with anger. "I've had three kids, and I can tell you there's nothing funny about lying there helpless, with your legs in stirrups. No man who took his hippocratic oath would make jokes like that."

"Oh," Genna murmured. "I think he took his *hypocritic* oath, all right."

"Tiffany," Nick leaned forward, "what's said in this room remains in this room. But we need to know. How far did you go with this supposed doctor."

"We always stayed around Chicago. I only ever had a couple of hours then I'd have to get back for the kids."

This woman was dumber than the tissue box she'd practically emptied. "Nick means, did you have sex with the man you knew as Dr. Ersatz," Genna clarified.

Tiffany's eyes welled again, and her blush heightened. "No. I love Rory. I—I just wanted to feel attractive again. I just wanted someone to listen... And Stephen—Dr. Ersatz—I mean, uh, this new man was so interested in me."

Or in your trust fund, Genna thought.

She glanced at Nick and found him watching her with his brows slightly raised. She gave a brief nod in answer to the unspoken question. Yes, she believed Tiffany Ross. Everything from the woman's body language to the halting way she'd told the tale made her seem truthful. Plus, she didn't seem bright enough to tell a convincing lie.

He gave a brief nod in return, and she knew he agreed with her assessment. Now it was a matter of pulling together all the information they could on the unfortunate non-affair.

"How long did you continue to see Dr.....ah, the doctor?" Nick asked.

"About six weeks, maybe two months," Tiffany answered, pulling a fresh tissue from the box.

"Where did you meet?"

"Usually at the coffee shop. Mostly we'd just talk. He was involved in groundbreaking research and told me how much he needed to raise money for his foundation. And how lonely he was."

Again her face brightened at the memory. "Once we went for lunch."

Genna was busy making notes. "Do you remember the name of the restaurant?"

She named an upscale eatery known for its intimate atmosphere.

"Did he pay by credit card?" Genna asked, wondering if there was a chance they could trace the man through the purchase.

There was a pause and Genna glanced up to find their client contemplating her manicure. "I paid," she admitted. "He said he'd forgotten his wallet when he changed back to his street clothes from his surgery scrubs."

"Do you have any idea who this guy is?" Nick asked.

"Why is it important?"

"We understand this is awkward for you, but your husband is suing for divorce based on adultery. The doctor is the only person who can corroborate your story that the two of you didn't have sex.''

She stared from one to the other, her eyes puddles of misery above smudged mascara. "His name's Simon Chance.''

"Good," Nick smiled at her. "That's great. How did you find out his real name?''

"Well, in the restaurant, after he'd had a couple of glasses of red wine, he started telling these stories— you know, about his patients. He just didn't sound like much of a doctor to talk about stuff like that over lunch. Then, when we'd eaten, he tried to talk me into going to a hotel with him. I guess, by then, I figured out he probably just wanted sex. I got a weird feeling. And, I admit, I was curious about him. After I dropped him back off at the hospital…''

"Go on," Nick encouraged. He had a way of making everything sound so reasonable.

Tiffany had all but forgotten Genna was there scribbling away. She had her body turned toward Nick and it was to him she told her story. Genna had always admired his talent for getting people to open up. *He* was a good listener, she realized.

"The whole thing was so crazy anyway, I decided to follow him.''

"Good for you," Nick praised.

And Genna thought, good for their case if Dr. Ersatz corroborated Tiffany's story.

"I dropped him back off at the hospital and drove away. We'd agreed to meet again for coffee, and he was really pushing the idea of going to a hotel. I said I'd think about it. But, like I said, I had this weird feeling. So, anyway, I doubled back and sure enough he came out of the hospital just a couple of minutes later and started walking. I followed him a few blocks. He got into a beat-up old car and drove to a walk-up apartment. It was kind of grungy where he lived. He parked in resident parking and went inside.''

"Then what did you do?"

"I found a spot on the street and waited, but he didn't come out. After a while I just couldn't stand it, so I got out of the car and went to the building. It had one of those panels outside with the names on it and a number to phone.'' She blushed and hung her head.

"No Dr. Ersatz?"

She shook her head. "I stood around for a while trying to get up the courage to ring the building manager, but then an older man came out of the building and held the door open for me.'' She glanced at Nick guiltily.

"I went in. I didn't think about what I was going to do. I just went in.'' She wrinkled her nose. "It was kind of smelly in there, like it didn't get cleaned very often. There was a bank of mailboxes and I went and read them, just in case…you know. Maybe he had a roommate or something and his name was on a mailbox.''

Nick nodded encouragement.

"There was no mailbox with his name on it. But there was a bulletin board with some notices. Things for sale, people looking for a roommate, you know? And there was this newspaper clipping pinned up there with his picture on it.''

"A wanted poster?'' Genna mumbled.

"No. It was a review of a play at a little theater I'd never heard of. Simon Chance was the name of the guy in the picture. Somebody had circled it in red felt and written, 'Way to go, Si.'"

Genna wrote, *Simon Chance. Two-bit actor.* "Do you remember the name of the play or the theater?"

"No. Sorry."

"Address of the apartment?"

Tiffany shook her head.

"Could you find the apartment again?"

"I think so."

"Good," Nick said. "That's a start. Did you see him again?"

"No. I wouldn't have anyway, but the day after we went for lunch my husband came home and told me he wanted a divorce." Her voice began to tremble. "He said he knew I'd been cheating on him. I tried to tell him the truth, but he wouldn't listen. He told me I'd be hearing from his lawyer." She grabbed another tissue. "And then he left."

Genna wrote *Husband intractable. Shows no signs of wanting reconciliation.*

"WELL?" NICK TURNED to Genna as soon as he'd shown Tiffany Ross out.

She was thumbing through her notes, a businesslike frown between her brows. "I'm guessing Simon Chance aka Dr. Ersatz is going to want cash."

"I mean about the case. Do we have one?"

She glanced up, a question in her eyes. He didn't care if there was a case or not. He just wanted to keep her talking, to be with her. Her blond hair caught the light and gleamed white-gold. He knew she kept it short for practicality, and yet it drove him crazy wanting to shove his fingers into its perky softness. To get it sticking out in all directions because she'd been thrashing her head against the pillow as he'd made love to her.

He'd been going crazy with the wanting. What a fool he'd been to think he could have her just once. Oh, hell. He'd never planned to have just one night. He'd assumed, with an egotism that staggered him now he thought about it, that once they'd made love, she'd demand more. She'd flip on a light switch and be thrilled to find that he was her mystery man. But, she hadn't.

Did she think of that one magical night as often as he did? It was tough to tell with Genna, she was always so controlled. He needed to sneak a peek behind that calm facade. And this case gave him an opportunity he couldn't resist.

"There's always a case if one party feels injured." She might as well have been quoting a textbook.

"But her so-called affair was no more than a fantasy." He emphasized the word fantasy with calm deliberation. "If it only existed in her head, who's to say what was real and what wasn't? That's the power of fantasy."

Genna's face remained cool and businesslike, but beneath her suit jacket her chest rose and fell with a jerk.

"If a man fantasizes about making love to another woman, is he unfaithful?"

"But Simon Chance wasn't a fantasy, he's a real guy. Scum, but breathing."

"Dr. Ersatz wasn't. He was a fictitious creation,

and yet he was as real to Mrs. Ross as...your whispering man in the garden.''

There was no doubting her reaction this time. She flushed scarlet and rose with a jerky motion, turning to stare out the window. "The two aren't the same at all," she muttered, and he heard more passion in her voice at that moment than he'd heard since their deeply passionate night together.

"Aren't they?"

She shook her head violently. "I wish I'd never told you about that. It was just a stupid episode, brought on by too much atmosphere and too many mint juleps."

He stared at her agitated profile. *Liar.* He wanted to walk up behind her and whisper the word into her ear. He wanted to turn her to him and kiss her until she admitted their night together had shaken her to the core just as it had him. He wanted her....

That was his problem in a nutshell. He wanted her. Damn it, it was more than a want. It was a need. The need to taste her flesh, to fill her body with his own almost consumed him. To make her admit that she was a flesh-and-blood woman, as full of passion as she was of business acumen.

He rose and took a step toward her, then stopped.

She was buttoning her suit jacket. Even a guy with psych 101 behind him could interpret the meaning behind that gesture. It wasn't cold that had her fastening those buttons. Her business jacket was her armor, defending her against unwanted intrusion into her personal life.

Her face was set in stubborn lines as she stared out the window. Nick watched her and his gut twisted.

She wasn't ready to face her own needs. She wasn't ready for him to make a move.

But was she really willing to pretend their affair in New Orleans was nothing but a crazy incident brought on by the location and a measly bit of alcohol consumption?

Only the fiercest act of will kept him from going to her, because he knew if he so much as touched her shoulder he'd be lost. Nothing would stop him until she knew he was the man she'd made love with in that darkened hotel room. And he had a dreadful suspicion that would be disaster. She wasn't ready to accept the truth. Not yet.

He might feel for her confusion, but he wasn't a damn saint, either. She was going to have to face up to her passionate nature some time soon.

And he was just the man to help her do it.

There ought to be a humanitarian award with his name on it!

At the moment, however, he could see Genna wasn't ready for anything more. Just the reminder of her experience in New Orleans had her staring out his office window intently, and he didn't think it was the statue of Ceres at the foot of La Salle Street that she was seeing. She was in some kind of zone all her own.

"Well, I guess that's a start," he said, and watched her jump as the sound of his voice broke into her reverie. "When you type up those notes, can you e-mail me a copy?"

"Hmm?" Her eyes appeared vague as she turned to him, like those of a woman waking from a dream. Slowly they sharpened as his words sank in and he could see the effort it took to return to the present. He didn't have to be a mind reader to know exactly where her thoughts had been.

It was a vision devoid of pictures. There was only touch, sound, taste and smell, and like two blind people, they had found those senses superheightened as they made love in the dark. He felt again her smooth silky flesh moving against his, heard her tiny cries, almost of distress, as her control slipped. Those cries changed to more gutteral sounds as she came, against his fingers, his mouth and around his thrusting cock.

He had to turn from her to disguise the way that cock was even now straining to get her attention. He moved rapidly to his desk and sat painfully behind it. "Your notes," he reminded her hoarsely.

"Right. I'll send them," she said. "See you later." And she walked slowly out of his office.

He watched her every step of the way, noting the slimness of her hips beneath the skirt, and, unable to help himself, he recalled how they felt gyrating beneath his thrusting body.

Raising his gaze didn't help. Then he saw the long, proud line of her back and remembered how it felt arching against him as she cried out deep in her throat.

Dropping his gaze lower was no more useful. There were her narrow feet in sensible low-heeled pumps. And all he could think about was how she'd giggled and sighed as he'd sucked on each separate toe. And later, how those toes had curled, clawlike, against his shoulders.

But the one thing he couldn't do was remove his gaze from her body completely. He wasn't released from her spell until she'd left. Still he stared at the partially open door for a moment before dropping his head in his hands.

He cursed quietly. Obsession seemed to be going around like the flu. Tiffany Ross had it, Genna had it, now he was showing all the symptoms.

Well, he wasn't going to wait around hoping Genna would come to her senses and face her inner sexpot. He was damn well going to do something that would help cure them both.

He sat there for a moment deep in thought, then dragged his computer keyboard toward him.

GENNA GOT TO her desk earlier than usual the next day. Her sleep had been hopelessly tormented by that hypnotic voice whispering to her deepest, darkest desires.

Again and again she'd woken, reaching for him— her nameless lover—and met empty air and tangled bedclothes. Groaning in want and frustration, she'd tried hot milk, a warm bath, she'd read a couple of chapters from an old college textbook on oceanography. It had put her to sleep often enough during the course, now it failed her. She no sooner read about bathythermograph—no doubt a useful word to have handy at a cocktail reception—than it seemed to her fevered brain as though his voice were whispering those words into her ear.

She had thrown the textbook across the room in total frustration, realizing with grim irony that she could have aced oceanography if she'd had that voice reading to her then. Ocean currents and temperature variations would have seemed as riveting as erotica.

Knowing sleep was beyond her, she'd finally climbed out of bed at four. She was the first one at the gym that morning, working out with punishing fierceness as though by disciplining her muscles relentlessly she could control her thoughts.

She'd had time for a sauna and a breakfast of yogurt and a muffin and was still the first one to arrive on her floor.

When she saw the envelope on her desk, her heart jumped from normal to fast and then extreme workout range, pounding itself into the stratosphere.

It was just a plain white envelope with her name and the words, *Personal and Confidential* typewritten on the front. But she knew it was from him. How she knew she couldn't have said. But yes, she could. The words were in the soft gray print the firm used for drafts, and they were italicized.

Her name was in the typewritten equivalent of a whisper.

Even though he'd never once whispered her name, she heard him do it now, deep in her psyche.

She found her legs were trembling so much she dropped her briefcase and slumped into her chair. Her hands also trembled as she reached for the envelope. It was sealed, and she imagined his tongue trailing wetness along the flap the way he'd trailed it along her lips that night. With a soft moan, she couldn't stop remembering the other places he'd trailed that wickedly clever tongue. And she began to burn and throb in every one of those places. And a few others he hadn't made it to.

Yet.

The "yet" was implied, wasn't it? Inside that

sealed envelope? He knew who she was, then. Somehow she wasn't surprised. She'd considered the possibility that he worked for her firm.

Perhaps she'd recognize him if she saw him in the light. Maybe his face would be familiar from the elevator, or in one of the many meetings she attended. A little shiver ran up her spine.

Tracing the outline of the lumpy rectangular envelope with one finger, she knew there was nothing inside for her but complication.

Complication she didn't need.

Just knowing he'd touched it gave her a strange thrill.

She dropped the thing on her desk and wiped her hands on her slacks. No, no, no.

Inside that envelope was lust. Wasted time she could never get back. Self-indulgence. *Pleasure.* With a sharp reminder to herself that she'd get enough pleasure when she joined the partners as the youngest ever, she picked up the envelope and tossed it, unopened, into the trash.

Where it remained for five of the worst minutes of her life.

It was like some kind of supermagnet, and she had as much resistance as an iron filing. What was in that envelope that caused it to bulge? What had he written to her? When she could stand it no longer, she grabbed the letter out of her trash bin and opened it.

There were two things inside. One was a single white page with no signature, no letterhead, nothing to distinguish it. As far as she could tell, the letter, in the same gray script as the envelope, could have come from any of the printers her firm used.

She took all this in as she scanned the sheet rapidly, then her gaze fell on the first words and she moaned helplessly.

I can't stop thinking about you.

You're not the only one, she thought.

Meet me at room 1604 at the Shaftsbury Hotel this Friday at 11:00 p.m. No lights—unless you want to see me.

Neptune.

Even her breath trembled as she finished reading the words.

The other item in the envelope was a pair of black cotton sports briefs that she recognized as the ones he'd "bought" during her striptease. Just holding them in her hand brought back that crazy, exciting night. She couldn't stop the cat-licking-the-cream smile those memories caused.

She pushed the panties to the bottom of her bag, glad she was early and no one had witnessed her opening her mail.

As she'd suspected, he knew who she was, but he'd signed his name Neptune, so presumably he was happy to continue the one-sided anonymity. And he promised her darkness: a cloak of secrecy that made her tingle with excitement.

If she showed up at the hotel would she be tempted to find out who he was?

What on earth was she thinking? Of course she wasn't going to show up Friday night. Apart from his insulting insinuation that she didn't have anything better to do, there was the small problem of her not having time for an affair. Not even an anonymous one.

With a jerky motion, she rose and stalked out to the closest document shredder and watched with satisfaction as she turned Neptune's letter into paper spaghetti.

Feeling refreshed and virtuous, she stomped back to her office and checked her Day-Timer. Hah, she was busy on Friday night. She was going to a Taiwanese movie with her friend Marcy.

Well then, that was that.

Of course, the curse of a photographic memory was that she could still see every word of the letter in her mind, including the room number and hotel name. But that didn't matter. She had mentally shredded the invitation just as surely as the mechanical device had.

5

"WHAT DID YOU THINK of the movie?"

"I didn't understand a word," Genna replied.

A bright laugh answered her. "It was in Taiwanese. You were supposed to read the subtitles."

There were subtitles? Who knew? All she knew was that her brain was telling her to drive straight home after the movie. Don't even *think* of turning up at a hotel to meet a stranger. But even as she scolded herself, she ached and throbbed in intimate places so fiercely that she could hardly sit still.

The arguments she'd had with herself all week only intensified as she sat watching the changing shapes on the screen, hearing the mumble of foreign voices, while a much more personal drama played out inside her head.

To go to the hotel was as good as admitting she wanted to start an affair with a man she'd seen only in a shiny gold mask and who called himself Neptune. And, if she turned up at a Chicago hotel for a pre-arranged assignation, she couldn't blame it on moonlight, mint juleps and magnolia. The very idea was trashy and stupid.

Stupid, foolhardy, self-indulgent, possibly even dangerous.

And still she throbbed with wanting him.

The silk underwear she'd been insane to slip into this evening were tantalizingly soft as she made her way up the theater aisle beside Marcy, inhaling the smell of popcorn as she breathed deeply to try to calm her racing heart.

A surreptitious glance at her watch showed it was just eleven now. Damn. Why couldn't the movie have been one of those four-hour seven-generational Chinese epics? She tried to slow her steps, but the post-movie stampede pushed her on.

"Do you feel like going somewhere for a drink?" she asked Marcy in a desperate bid to stall for time.

From the odd expression on her friend's face, and the fact that her mouth was already open, she realized she'd interrupted her. She'd probably been analyzing the movie.

"Sorry to interrupt," she said with a guilty smile, "but it's so hard to hear with all this noise." She gestured to the babbling throng.

Marcy narrowed her eyes. "Are you feeling all right?"

"Yes. I just feel like going out for a drink."

"I was in the middle of telling you I have to get right back home. I've got an early squash game tomorrow." Marcy's kindly round face creased in a worried frown. "But I guess I could go for a quick one if you need to talk about something."

God, she felt like a moron. "Sorry. Couldn't hear. No, that's fine. Go on home. We'll catch up some other time."

She tried to keep up a light conversation while she drove her friend home, but she could barely form a coherent sentence, or comprehend a thing Marcy said.

I won't go.

I need to go.

Back and forth went the endless seesaw argument. Head over heart—or lust over brain—again and again. When Genna dropped Marcy at her place, she was mentally exhausted from the struggle.

Her friend turned to her before getting out of the car, and the dashboard lights illuminated a worried frown on Marcy's face. "Want to come in for coffee or something? You seem kind of twitchy. I know there's something on your mind."

Wrong. Her mind had nothing to do with it.

"No. I'm not going to be responsible if you lose your game tomorrow." Marcy had her sights set on being club champion. "Good luck."

"Same to you."

She waved as Marcy entered her building, then pulled away from the curb.

Suddenly, it was as if she were cast in her own horror movie. Her mind insisted she head straight home, but a demon had possessed her body and refused to obey.

I won't go.

I need to go.

Sweat broke out on her forehead at the mental and physical struggle, but it was hopeless. Her body might have been taken over by a sex-starved alien for all the control she seemed able to exert. Where was her famous self-discipline when she needed it most?

Her personal global positioning system seemed to guide her to the Shaftsbury Hotel without any effort at all. She pulled up to the entrance with a jerk as her foot stamped the brake like a kid having a temper tantrum. Even as she handed her keys to a valet she wondered if she'd really go to room 1604.

The lobby felt huge and anonymous, and her shoes clacked across the marble foyer making her feel utterly conspicuous. Not that it was exactly hopping at—she glanced at her watch—eleven forty-five at night.

"Evening, ma'am," a bellhop greeted her.

"Evening," she tried to smile.

"Can I help you with anything?"

I'm just here to have sex, thanks. "No, thank you. I have everything I need."

Except a brain. Her steps slowed as she approached the elevator. She didn't have a clue what she was doing here. Chances were her mystery lover had left by now anyway. She was seriously late.

Still, she entered the elevator and pushed the button, taking a deep breath in an effort to slow her pounding heart. She wished she knew of a breathing exercise that would give her some relief from the ache between her legs.

Before she knew it, she was standing in front of room 1604. She rested her fingertips lightly on the blond wood of the door and saw them tremble.

Was he in there? Was he thinking about her? Wondering if she'd show? Was he watching TV? Sound asleep?

Or had he given up on her and left?

That's what she should do. Leave.

But she didn't. Her right hand rose, almost as though it didn't belong to her, formed itself into a tight fist, and rapped on the door.

Now that she'd made her decision, her breasts tingled in anticipation of being with him again. A minute passed and she felt her nipples tighten almost painfully. Two minutes and with dawning dread it occurred to her that he might actually have left.

Her vanity took a nosedive.

So much for "I can't stop thinking about you." He couldn't wait—she checked her watch again—fortyeight minutes? She stared at the door, regret a lead weight in her stomach.

Now that it was too late she knew beyond any doubt how much she needed him right now, this stranger who had the power to summon her, to make her act crazy. And he hadn't waited so much as an hour for her.

What was she going to do? She had no way to contact him, to tell him she wanted to see him again. With a little huff of disappointment, she turned to leave.

But, just as she turned away, she heard the latch.

She turned back and watched the door open slowly.

Into utter darkness.

Light spilled from the hallway a couple of feet into the room, but there was no one standing in the light. He must be behind the door.

A chill of nerves skittered across her stomach as she paused, uncertain once again, on the threshold.

"Come in." That oh-so-familiar whisper drew her forward as surely as if he'd tied a rope to her and pulled.

She hesitated a moment on the brink, then crossed into the dark room and he closed the door behind her. Her eyes hadn't had time to acclimatize to the darkness, so all she saw was a vague shape of a man. Then the door clicked shut and she saw nothing.

"I can't stay," she sputtered, as sanity tried once again to override her crazy impulses.

"It was nice of you to come and tell me in person." Was that a smile she heard in his voice? Hard to tell with a whisper.

"I...thank you for the invitation. But I can't stay." She'd forgotten how it felt to be in utter darkness with a man she didn't know. The thickest blindfold wouldn't have made this room any blacker.

"May I ask why?" He was so courteous, so formal. He didn't smother her with kisses or so much as touch her. As far as she could tell he hadn't moved. Which was a good thing. Of course she didn't want to be lunged at and manhandled the minute she walked through the doorway.

Even as her body yearned for him, she said, "I...I just don't think this is a good idea."

"You're afraid." He said it matter-of-factly, as though he expected her to bolt.

She was more than afraid. She was terrified. But no midnight Romeo was going to know that. "Of course I'm not afraid."

"Yes, you are. I can hear it in your tone. I can feel you tremble from here."

She sucked in a startled breath, so conscious of his presence, so very confused by her own outlandish reaction. He was just a guy. Any man and no man. He had no identity, so why should he throw her off balance this way?

"Or maybe it's not entirely fear." He touched her. She couldn't prevent a gasp as his hand brushed lightly over her collarbone, skimming down over her breast, which seemed to bloom against the pressure of his palm.

"Ah," he murmured. "Not entirely fear, is it?"

Fear or desire? She wasn't sure herself which emotion was more prevalent. But, whichever it was, sleeping with him was still a bad idea. He'd made it clear he knew who she was while she knew nothing about him, except that he most likely worked at the same firm. She was literally putting her career in his hands. She could never be this reckless with her future.

But her breasts thought it was a very good idea to be in his hands, as did other parts of her anatomy, and they were all doing their best to drown her sensible thoughts.

"I don't want to sleep with you," she managed to blurt in a voice that sounded soft and husky.

"We don't have to sleep," he promised, his other hand stroking her neck. The trembling was spreading now, every part of her body weakening with it.

"I meant—"

"Trust me." His voice, as soft as a purr, seemed to hypnotize her almost as much as the steady stroking of his hands. "Stay for just a little while."

A kind of humming sound came from her lips.

He kissed her. It was so dark she didn't see it coming, and gasped at the intimate shock as his lips covered hers, warm and sure. Again that humming noise came from her lips; it seemed the only communication she was capable of.

He understood her wordless plea and wrapped his arms firmly around her, pulling her against his body. Her clinging hands felt terry towel, and she realized he was wearing a hotel robe. She had a strong suspicion there was nothing under it, and all at once her own clothing felt like armor, thick and heavy. Suffocating.

"The other night was a mistake," she said, managing to break away from his mouth, trying to make herself heard above the pounding of her heart. "I never do things like this."

"I know," he soothed. "It's okay."

His lips came back to hers, softly at first, almost teasing in their softness. Light brushing kisses that made her want more. And then he gave her more, entering her mouth with his hot, wet tongue, stroking her mouth, forcing her to respond.

His kisses lured her on, deeper into the room, one shuffling step at a time in an oddly intimate dance. She should have felt accustomed to the utter darkness by now, but it still felt as erotically foreign as it had that night in New Orleans. It could have been a continuation—hell, in this dark hotel room she could *be* in New Orleans, or anywhere else in the world for that matter.

No. Something about the atmosphere was evocative of that amazing night in Louisiana. Another deep, drugging kiss, another step and she felt the edge of the bed against the back of her legs. A little quiver, a mixture of desire and dread, traveled along her coiled nerves.

Just as she opened her mouth to stop this thing from going any further, his pressing warmth was gone. Another little sound, embarrassingly like a whimper, escaped her lips.

Then she gasped as she felt something soft and cool

trace her cheekbone and slide slowly across her lips. "Magnolia," she sighed the word as she inhaled the scent. No wonder she'd been reminded of New Orleans.

"You're trying to seduce me with memories," she said softly, wishing it wasn't working quite so effectively.

"Do you need to be reminded?" he whispered, his lips all but touching her ear.

No. She didn't. She didn't need to be seduced, either. Her memories did that all by themselves. Those memories haunted her dreams, interrupted her waking thoughts. The scent merely intensified the wanting, and she wanted him desperately even as her mind struggled against her desire.

She breathed deeply of the exotic perfume and felt its essence invade her body like a drug that both soothed and excited.

His tongue trailed a slow, wet circle around her ear, the velvety texture of his tongue brushing the sensitive skin of her ear.

The magnolia blossom followed the path of his tongue as the cool petals traveled over the damp, sensitive skin, sending shivers through her body.

He thrust the stem into her hair so the bloom rested atop her ear, making her feel like a lush Tahitian native in a Gauguin painting. Except she should be wearing a sarong, not the burden of her western, corporate, conservative, extremely constricting clothing.

Her sleeveless cotton sweater felt so heavy against her breasts it was an effort to breathe.

As though he'd read her mind, his hands moved to trace the line of buttons down her front. Then, instead of yanking the sweater open as she wished, so the buttons popped and flew in a dozen directions, those light fingers traced the waistband of her slacks. They dropped with devastating softness to her belly where they did nothing but follow the line of her fly.

But, of course, he hadn't seen her. He had no idea what she was wearing, so he'd used his fingers to discover his path to undressing her. Again she felt the erotic thrill of darkness surrounding her, pressing against her like a blanket. She now understood the term "under cover of darkness" as she never had before. She felt cloaked by it, invisible, as though what went on in this room wouldn't count in the real world. Her world—the world of fluorescent lights and the constant scrutiny of facts, arguments, details— was blotted out.

Under cover of darkness she was free to be and do whatever she desired. And whatever her whispering stranger desired.

She was living a potent sexual fantasy. She sighed and let her head fall back.

Those light, sure fingers traced their way back up the buttons to pause at the very top. She felt her breath halt as he slipped the first one free, felt the brushing roughness of his fingertips against the flesh of her neck and along the curve of her collarbone.

"I wasn't sure you'd come," he whispered, the breath stirring the hair on top of her head.

"I didn't plan to. Didn't want to."

"But you're here," he pointed out as the second button slid free.

"I should go," she said, but it sounded weak and pitiful in her own ears.

"We'll stop whenever you say the word," he promised.

And she believed him. Why, she couldn't have said. It was instinct. Or maybe it was the gentle way he treated her, the way he seemed to understand her fears and objections.

She was a great fool, but it felt wonderful to do something completely foolish for the first time in her life.

He finished the buttons and peeled back the sides of her sweater, revealing the plunging satin bra that he couldn't see. He couldn't know it made her look like a naughty French postcard. He could feel it, though, and he did, taking his sweet time, taunting her nipples until she feared they'd burst through the silk like twin bullets.

"I like this," he murmured. "What color is it?"

"Mauve."

"I bet it looks great against your skin."

"It does," she assured him, remembering the secret thrill she'd experienced when she checked out her reflection earlier that evening. When she'd dressed in purple silk lingerie to see a movie with a woman friend. She now accepted that she'd lost the argument with herself the moment she slit open the envelope that contained his invitation. From that moment she'd been drawn inexorably to this meeting.

"I bet it looks better off." He reached behind her, slipped open the clasp and removed the wispy thing.

If breasts could sigh, hers would have as they fell free, straining eagerly for his touch. She wondered what form it would take as her whole body tried to see him in the dark.

His touch came, but it was a hot, wet assault she hadn't expected, when she felt his mouth on her breast, not his fingers. And because she wasn't prepared, she had no defense ready.

The last of her resistance melted under his hot tongue. She clutched his head, her fingers curling into the soft, springing hair, her own head thrown back as sensation bombarded her.

His tongue curled around a nipple, which she knew without sight was clenched tight and hard with desire. He licked and teased, then sucked on her so hard she gasped. Once more he soothed her, his tongue swirling round her engorged nipple. He scraped the sensitive flesh with his teeth and, as she drew in her breath tensing for the sharp nip, he again surprised her with soft suckling. First one, then the other breast.

While his mouth was busy so were his hands, divesting her of her slacks so deftly she barely noticed the slide of linen over her hips and down her legs.

Now, she wore nothing but mauve satin tap pants. She could be tortured on the rack and she'd never admit she'd bought them thinking of his hand being free to travel up that pant leg unobstructed by elastic. But when that hand did travel upward, she sighed with soft pleasure.

Even though he started at the back.

He dropped to his knees before her. His finger traced the curving line of her bottom then slipped up to caress a cheek. As his hand feathered over the crease between her cheeks she felt an odd fluttering and knew she'd just broken out in goose bumps.

"Your ass is as beautiful as your breasts," he told her, his breath warm against her hip. He squeezed and kneaded the flesh for a few minutes, making the satin pull against her crotch in a rhythm that had her shuddering. He was tormenting her, she knew, yet she couldn't stop her body from responding. His breath was warm and moist against her pubis as he knelt before her, tantalizingly close, so all she could think about was having his mouth on her. But he made her wait. Building up her pleasure so slowly it was almost painful.

As his breath wafted against her, it felt cool, and she blushed in the darkness knowing it was because her own wetness had soaked the satin. Again, she wondered if he'd read her mind, or at least divined the direction of her thoughts, for his hands slipped out of her panties and this time he traced her shape from the outside. Starting at the silky waistband in back, he followed the crease of her bottom with his index finger, pausing at the spot she knew was soaked with her juices.

"You liked that," he said.

"Yes." Her voice trembled as she waited for that finger to continue its journey to where she needed it most. But it stayed put, increasing in pressure so she felt him at the entrance to her vagina, the damp silk clinging to his finger.

"Spread your legs a little more," he said.

They felt so boneless she wasn't sure they'd support her, but she did as he asked, clutching his shoulders for balance and opening herself to him. The pressure increased and she felt the slight abrasion of the satin as it entered her, scraping her skin lightly as it absorbed her moisture. He didn't push it in far, just enough to remind her of how empty she felt and to make her throb from wanting him to fill her.

Her legs were beginning to tremble and still he hadn't touched her where she most wanted to be touched. Oh, his breath was hot against that spot, though, driving her wild on the other side of the satin barrier. Her hands tried to pull his head forward, but, with a quiet chuckle, he refused to be moved.

He withdrew his finger and pulled her panties off, then pushed her back so she was lying on the bed. She slipped off her sandals and heard them plop to the carpet.

She heard the tearing of a condom package and felt the movement beside her as he sheathed himself.

The mattress shifted so at least she had some warning before she rolled against his body, although she still suffered a slight shock as she bumped into warm male skin. Very hard and very hot. He'd obviously stripped off his robe, and as he rolled up against her, she felt the jut of his penis against her hip. As she'd suspected, he'd been naked under the robe all along.

Why that made her feel even warmer, she couldn't have said. She seemed ultrasensitive to every nuance, her imagination as supersensitized as her skin. From head to toe she was one big, throbbing need and the filler of that need was here beside her.

She wanted him.

Inside her.

Now!

She felt his hands on her bare shoulder, his lips at her throat.

She wondered if he could feel her purring.

Her own hands started to wander, tracing warm skin, tangling with curly hair.

His hand was on her knee, her inner thigh, moving up. Moving up. *Oh, yes.* He cupped her intimately, pressing his palm against her as though checking for fever. Which she definitely had. Raging fever. Thermometer-shattering fever.

He slid one finger inside her, then two, rubbing and stretching until she rocked her hips to his rhythm. If he was trying to keep her on simmer until she burned dry, he was doing a great job.

Should she give him a hint to pick up the pace a bit? Trouble was, she didn't know him. Not even his name or what he looked like. Still, he was as close to a fantasy come to life as she was ever going to get. Her fantasy, her rules.

"I want you to touch me," she whispered.

"Where?" he whispered back, and damn if she didn't hear the laugh in his voice. He was playing with her. Deliberately. Sadist.

"Here!" She dragged his hand out of her body and stuck it in the general vicinity of her hot button.

"You mean here?"

All that came out of her mouth was a combination between a sigh and a grunt. She was incapable of speech. He'd found it all right. He held that exquisitely sensitive nub between his thumb and forefinger.

Oh, she was so close. So marvelously close. The excitement built as she waited for his fingers to start moving, giving her the orgasm that trembled on the edge.

He didn't move at all. Just held her, applying

enough pressure that she felt the pinch—not pain, just intense sensation.

Hours seemed to pass.

Sweat beaded on her forehead and words, cries, appeals crowded in her throat like a logjam so nothing coherent could emerge. She moved her hips, desperate to get some friction, some relief from the relentlessly building pressure, but his hand just followed the motions of her hips—refusing her the release her whole body begged for.

Undulating turned to thrashing and still he just held her, all that exquisitely sensitive flesh imprisoned between his squeezing thumb and finger.

It was torture. He was killing her. And yet, she'd never felt so alive.

"I want to tell you a story," he whispered in her ear. "A bedtime story." He leaned forward to kiss her damp forehead, the pressure on her trapped clit increasing slightly as he moved.

She whimpered.

"Shh. Bedtime stories should soothe."

That was it. She was going to kill him. She was damn well going to kill him.

If she survived this sexual torture.

"The story is about a princess who lived long ago in a faraway land." His words were soothingly hypnotic, his voice soft and relaxed, completely at odds with the relentless firmness of his fingers.

"Like most fairy-tale princesses, she was beautiful and virtuous, but she had one fatal flaw. Do you know what it was?"

She gasped.

"Her fatal flaw was that she didn't know how to

give up control. Not ever. She excelled at everything she put her mind to. Everything from embroidery to archery to dancing and…whatever things princesses do.''

Her brain was so fogged with frustrated desire, she could barely take in the words. She just wished she had control over her own body at this moment. She was so close, so painfully close, it was killing her. The pressure was building so much she felt she would blow apart any second.

''Since she was a princess and amazingly cute and sexy, princes came from far and wide to beg for her hand in marriage. But she spurned them all. She said she was quite happy in her own kingdom where she was in charge. But one prince could see inside her heart. He knew she was lonely.''

He paused the story long enough to kiss her breasts, licking the sensitive nipples and tracing the undersides with his tongue. Wildly, she hoped this was it and he'd shut up with the fairy tales and get on with the business at hand. The business trapped so helplessly in his right hand.

But he didn't. His dratted fingers never moved. She jerked her hips, hoping to catch him off guard and get a little friction going. He merely chuckled, and his tongue caressing her breasts only added an extra layer of helpless frustration.

His mouth cruised back to her ear, stopping to taste and nibble his way until his head was again beside her on the pillow, his whisper an intimate caress against her ear. ''Where was I?''

''Please,'' she whispered hoarsely, hating herself

for begging but knowing she couldn't take much more.

He kissed her, a light feathery kiss that just brushed her lips.

"Ah, yes, the prince. He knew he had to teach the princess that it was okay to give up control once in a while. That she could be as strong, or stronger, with the right mate. He knew there was only one way to do that. He had to teach her to want him as a woman wants a man. He had to teach her pleasure. But first he had to get her alone. Do you know what he did?"

In spite of herself, she was intrigued. This sounded like a very grown-up fairy tale, nothing like the ones she remembered as a kid with the gently sweet drawings. Since she was currently incapable of speech, she shook her head.

"The prince kidnapped his princess and took her to his castle where he kept her locked in a secret room in a tower." If anything, his whisper grew softer. "She was completely in his power."

In spite of herself, Genna shivered at the deliberate parallels he'd created between his "fairy tale" and this situation. She was alone with this man in a hotel tower. And she was in his power all right. Firmly in his grip, as his blasted fingers reminded her every throbbing second.

"What did he do to her?" she gasped.

"He kissed her when she pleased him. But sometimes he punished her."

"How did he punish her?" Her voice was husky, she couldn't take much more.

"He made her beg. He took control of her body and then he made her beg him to pleasure her."

"That is a very sick fairy tale," she informed him, biting her own lips to stop herself from begging this man who was certainly no prince.

"I don't think so. They lived happily ever after."

She groaned.

"That story didn't seem to relax you at all. Maybe I should try massage."

"Oh, yes." Her heart was pounding so she could barely breathe. And she felt the wetness of her unfulfilled desire sticky between her thighs.

"What's the magic word?" he taunted.

She wouldn't do it. She wouldn't give him the satisfaction.

He increased the pressure ever so slightly and her body squirmed. She couldn't hold out any longer. "Please!" she begged.

He gathered her wrists into his left hand and held them over her head as he swung his body over hers. He held himself poised over her throbbing vagina which wept with need. "Did I tell you he sometimes tied her up when he punished her?"

With a strangled cry, her hips jerked up toward where she felt him hovering in the darkness, his hardness pressing against her entrance. He released the pressure, leaving one finger on that engorged and tortured spot, and he plunged inside.

The cry came from somewhere deep inside her.

This, she thought, is how volcanoes erupt. The hot wet pressure had built and swelled behind the barrier, but now it burst free in hot torrents. She wrapped her legs around his hips and raised herself to meet his powerful thrusts. Oh, how he filled her, claimed her, drove her up and up.

The climax swamped her, wave after wave, while her body jerked and writhed completely out of control. He captured her cries in his mouth, except the last one, when he joined her with his own groan of release.

Every part of her was clasped around him, and against their pressed chests she heard her heart beat so frantically she was amazed she'd even survived.

Slowly, slowly, the waves ebbed to soothing ripples and her breathing approached normal. She felt drained, empty, and at the same time curiously full. That little incident had been more than just sex, and when she could think again, she'd ponder it at length.

SHE WAS TOO QUIET. Damn, Nick resented the darkness that hid Genna's expression. Had she understood what he was trying to tell her?

It was a simple message. He was trying to tell her that she needed him.

Of course, she hadn't yet recognized that her mystery guy and her work pal Nick were one and the same, but he knew now what he'd only hoped before. She needed him. All of him. She was too sexual a woman to deny herself as she'd been doing. She had to learn to give up her much-vaunted control and let go once in a while. Before it was too late and she no longer could.

It wasn't just in bed, either. She worked so hard at being strong and independent, she'd lost sight of the need to share things, to lean sometimes. He smiled smugly in the dark. It had just about driven her crazy to have him hold her on the edge like that without letting her come.

Good thing it was too dark for her to see the smirk he hadn't had to hide as he'd held her beneath him, feeling her frustration rise.

Once in a while helpless was good. When it was Genna who was helpless, and he was the one holding the reins, it was very, very good. Of course, it was possible he'd only succeeded in making her hate him, and this very promising secret affair might be abruptly terminated.

It was a chance he'd gladly take if there was also an equal chance he could break through all the barriers she'd erected around herself.

This affair was just perfect for Genna, he knew. He didn't exist for her outside this room. Unlike every other woman he'd ever known, she hated the complications a real relationship required. She didn't want personal phone calls at the office—she didn't have room on her billing chart.

He recalled a day that some poor schmo sent her flowers and she'd put them in the coffee room claiming they cluttered up her desk.

Time and efficiency were everything to her, but the sad thing was, she was squandering her best years in search of a partnership that sure as hell wouldn't keep her warm at night or sit rocking with her on her front porch in old age.

Beside him she flopped on her back sounding as if she'd just finished a triathlon. Her breath came in ragged gasps and heat emanated from her in waves.

He waited for her to speak, wondering what was going on in her mind.

"If you ever do that to me again, I'll—" she finally managed to gasp.

He grinned at her in the dark. "You'll what?"

"I'll think of something."

There was a long silence and then a muffled chuckle. There was another moment of silence while he waited for her to share the joke. "What?" he finally asked.

"I'm thinking," she said in a smug tone that had him narrowing his eyes in suspicion.

"Thinking what?"

Then he heard another sound, it was her hand patting along the night table. He heard the moment she found what she was looking for—a studly supply of condoms he'd piled there. If Genna had round two in mind, he liked the direction her thinking had taken.

He felt himself stir with renewed excitement.

There was no pillow talk of any kind, which he'd kind of expected, given the pointed fairy tale. Maybe she'd missed the significance, or just didn't feel like talking. Fine by him. Especially now that her hands were exploring his chest.

Her mouth soon got involved, too, burrowing through his chest hair until she found his nipples, which she then proceeded to torment with her tongue and teeth. She continued her lazy inspection, caressing his body. Most likely, she was giving him time to recuperate for the round two she so clearly had in mind.

He felt like telling her he was all recouped, thanks all the same. He was achingly ready and as randy as a teenager. Still, her exploring hands and mouth felt good. More than good. He relaxed, as much as a man with a throbbing boner could relax, and let her have her way.

Her hair tickled his sides, where he'd always been ticklish, but her exploring tongue felt so sexy he didn't care. He just lay back and gave into her, wondering where he'd feel her touch next.

Still, she managed to shock him when he felt her lips nuzzling his balls, then her tongue stroking them. When she took one gently into her mouth, he couldn't stop the grunt of pleasure as she swirled her tongue around his flesh, her mouth hot and wet. He waited for her to take his cock in her mouth, already half crazy with anticipation.

But first she insisted on treating his other ball to the same treatment, and damn, she took her time with it.

That silken tongue on his cock didn't materialize. Instead she put her firm little hands on him, stroking and rubbing. He knew he'd never be able to watch her with a pen in her hands again without reliving this moment.

He felt her soft hair brushing his inner thighs as she worked her tongue on his balls while her hands stroked and toyed with him. He sensed she needed to take control this round, and, after making her give it up so spectacularly a few minutes ago, he was happy to take his turn.

Until she got nasty.

She worked him up to a fine head of steam and he knew he was getting ready to explode. But he wanted to be inside her when it happened. "Honey, I'm going to—" She squeezed him deftly and a low moan cut off his words. "Get a condom," he managed. He'd forgotten to whisper, but his voice was so low and hoarse he doubted he sounded like anyone either of them knew.

"No, you're not going to come," she said with a voice so softly goading that he knew he was in trouble. "Not anytime soon."

He felt her body shift positions so she was kneeling over him, a hand replacing her mouth on his scrotum, not rubbing so much as gauging how close he was. She could have just asked him. He was so damn close, explosion was imminent.

Of their own volition, his hips started to thrust. He tried to hold back, wanting to be inside her but it was too—

Just as the moment of no return was upon him, her hand clamped him like a vise just below the head of his penis. She held him like that, calmly and firmly, until the surging tide inside him ebbed. "Aah," he cried out in shocked frustration.

He felt like calling her names. Like using his strength to flip her on her back and show her who was boss. The worst part was, he knew damn well there was a superior smirk on her face right now, just as there'd been on his face earlier.

It was payback time.

Well, she could have her fun, and her revenge, but there was one thing he sure as hell wouldn't do.

He wouldn't beg.

Those witch's fingers of hers started moving again, softly caressing, now firmly stoking him up and up— *Oh, yes, baby, yes*—and clamping him again so his hips bucked in torment. "Son of a—"

"Be nice. I want to tell you a bedtime story," she cooed, her firm grip cutting off his pleasure.

"There was once a prince who thought to torment his princess. Fortunately, she discovered her own power was no less than his." She leaned down and he felt the acute torment of her lips brushing the aching tip of his cock. Just above where her fingers held him captive. "Every time he punished her, she punished him right back."

If he wasn't in so damn much agony, he would have smiled at her perkiness.

He breathed deeply when she removed her hands and then the ache in his loins intensified when he heard the rip of a condom packet.

"What do you suppose happened?" she asked him, as she swiftly sheathed him.

"They burned her at the stake?" he managed to croak.

She laughed softly, and he felt the brush of her knee against his abdomen as she straddled him.

"No. He learned to be very, very nice to her in future."

He groaned as he felt her hovering above him.

"He learned good manners. Like please and thank you."

She brushed her wetness across his tip and he knew he was lost.

"Please," he muttered, knowing he'd give her anything. Beg all night, anything to thrust inside her glorious body and find his release.

She kissed his lips. "Once he learned his manners, they lived happily..." She impaled herself on him, taking him deep into her hot, lush body. He heard her gasp of delight even as his own moan shook him.

"Ever..." She pulled up torturously slowly, until

only his tip remained inside her. He felt her tight and quivering.

"After." She thrust down even as he arched up, striving to drive deeper still. She clung there for a moment unmoving, and the way her muscles tightened around him reminded him of her hand clamping on him, preventing his ejaculation. But these muscles didn't stop him, they spurred him on, massaging him until he exploded.

She cried out, her body bucking helplessly, each erotic contraction leading him to spurt after spurt of ecstasy.

She collapsed, damp and spent, against his chest, their bodies still joined, tucking her head under his chin.

He wrapped his arms around her and held on tight, feeling her, so fragile and yet so strong.

A little sigh lifted his chest hair, then another. Her body seemed to soften and grow heavier.

He continued to hold her against him while she slept.

The dueling fairy tales told him one thing. They were both enchanted. But what were the chances this thing could end in happily ever after?

6

GENNA WAS SO HOT.

The covers were too tight. She couldn't breathe. She opened her eyes to peer at the bedside clock and had the shock of waking in a strange place.

The bedside clock wasn't the right shape and she was confined, not by the bedclothes, but the arms of a naked man. It was his body, curled against hers, making her feel so hot.

Four-thirty in the morning, the LED display informed her. She could snuggle back in her lover's arms and go back to sleep.... Maybe they'd make love again in the morning. Sleepy, Saturday morning love.

With a sigh of anticipation, she snuggled back against him, feeling a flicker of desire as her back end pressed against his warmly sleeping belly. They could eat breakfast together.

Breakfast. A frown creased her forehead.

Daylight. Her eyes opened.

Discovery. She gasped. No way, no how.

As her mind awakened fully, she realized how foolish she'd been to fall asleep here in this hotel bed. Not that she'd intended to, of course, but she'd been drowsy after all that loving, and it had felt so good to curl up against him and close her eyes.

She had to remember this wasn't a normal affair she'd embarked on; it was a secret fantasy that would be dispelled by daylight. Like—she cudgeled her brain—Cupid and somebody. They'd had a gay old time until the woman...what was her name? Psyche. That was it. Psyche had broken the rules and looked at her sleeping lover's face. Then she'd lost him.

Goose bumps danced up Genna's spine. Thank goodness she'd woken. Now she had to get out of here. Because, like Psyche, part of her wanted to know who this man was. Even as a stronger voice within her warned her not to tempt fate.

She reached over in the dark and let her hands stroke his hair. He was so deeply asleep the slow rhythm of his breathing didn't change when she touched him. Her hands stalled as an idea struck her. She could flick on the light just long enough to see his face, just long enough to satisfy her curiosity. Would she recognize him vaguely or was he a complete stranger?

It wouldn't change anything if he didn't know she knew.

But she'd know.

Her hand stretched slowly toward the bedside lamp, fingers trembling. Her hand brushed the lampshade, reached under. Her fingers touched the light switch, then halted.

Did she really want to know? Now that she was fully awake, the myth came back to her. Cupid and Psyche. Psyche never saw her husband's face and was warned that if she did see him their happiness would end.

The remembered myth seemed chillingly prophetic.

Once Genna knew her sleeping lover's identity, her delightful fantasy would be over. Even if he never knew she knew, nothing could be the same. He could be somebody she didn't respect or even like. She could find herself staring across a boardroom table at him in a meeting and realize that outside the bedroom the man was an idiot. What a disappointment that would be.

No. It wasn't worth the risk. He was much more intriguing as a fantasy. He looked like whatever she wanted him to look like. Mel Gibson or Denzel Washington. She grinned to herself. Why choose? Denzel and Mel could alternate Fridays. He was ethical, funny, brilliant. He was anything she wanted him to be. She drew back her hand. For now, she'd trust him to keep their secret. She'd trust that he'd do nothing to hurt her career—or her.

She slipped out of bed and hunted for her clothes and sandals by feel. Once dressed, she crossed the room using the wall as her guide. As her hand grasped the cool metal of the door handle, she paused.

What if he misunderstood her middle-of-the-night escape?

What if he didn't contact her again?

The very thought made her heart pound and she almost hit the light switch just to be certain she could recognize him in future. But something stopped her again. The same internal shudder, part dread, part excitement. She stood uncertainly by the door for a second, thinking rapidly, then reached into her handbag for a notepad and pen.

She'd never written a note in the pitch dark before.

It would probably look like a little kid's writing. She decided to keep her message as simple as a child's.

I want to see you again. She wrote carefully, holding her thumb across the notebook page to give her pen some kind of guide. Then she moved her thumb down about half an inch and wrote a second line.

Same time next week. She frowned, not wanting him to think she expected him to pay. She was a modern woman. She moved her thumb down another half inch and wrote: *I'll book the room.* She signed it simply, *G.*

The ripping paper sounded loud in the silence, but she suspected it would take a jackhammer pounding in his ear to wake her lover. She'd exhausted him all right. She smiled in the dark feeling awfully pleased with herself as she crept back to drop the note on the bedside table.

Unable to resist, she bent and gave her sleeping lover a quick kiss on the cheek, feeling the scrape of new-grown whiskers against her lips.

He never moved. Not when she kissed him and not when she quietly let herself out of the room.

Was she crazy? she wondered as she drove through the early morning quiet streets of Chicago. Had she completely lost her mind?

Probably.

Did she care?

Not at the moment. Her car radio was set to an all-news station, but it just didn't match her mood, so she scanned until she came to an oldies rock and roll classic. "She loves you, yeah, yeah, yeah..." She belted out along with John, Paul, George and Ringo, except she changed the lyrics to "He loves me, yeah,

yeah, yeah,'' feeling as immature as a high-school sophomore in the throes of her first crush.

She remembered the way he'd held her, enthralled her, tormented her and finally surrendered to her own torment. It had been erotic, wilder than anything she'd ever done.

Why had she done it?

A slow smile formed. Because it had been fun.

''With a love like that, you know you should be glad. Yeah, yeah, yeah...'' She yelled out the words, feeling wild and free.

Reckless.

She'd gone to that hotel room because it had been reckless. Because she was twenty-eight years old and if she didn't do something reckless soon it would be too late.

She jerked to a halt as a light turned red and stopped singing. Whoa! Where had that notion come from?

Too late?

Once the light turned green, she pulled into a coffee place and grabbed a latte to go.

Drinking deeply, enjoying the hit of caffeine, she realized she was overtired and keyed up from her adventure. Now that she had the craziness out of her system, and a date for next week, there was no need to waste any more time in fantasy land.

Of course she wasn't too late. What she'd be too late for, if she wasn't careful, was her date with herself to make partner at her firm. She snapped the radio back to her twenty-four-hour all-news station.

As she made a mental list of everything she wanted to accomplish today, she realized she hadn't worked out in a few days. She tried to calculate how much time she wasted getting to and from the gym. Maybe she should buy one of those home-gym machines.

But she didn't have time to research them and shop for the right machine. And she didn't have a place to put it in her Lincoln Park loft, so she gave up on that idea. Maybe she could work out longer and go fewer days a week, she thought, as she pulled into her building's secured parking.

She could think better in her own place, and sighed with contentment as she climbed the four floors to her apartment. She loved her loft, part of a converted factory with fourteen-foot ceilings, exposed pipes, steel girders and wooden pillars.

Industrial chic, she called it. She'd bought it herself, decorated it herself, and she loved to clean it herself.

She didn't, however, love the part where she was on her own for maintenance and repairs. The first thing she did when she let herself in was check the bucket under her sink. It was half full, so the leak wasn't any worse. Still, she'd have to remind Nick of his promise to fix it for her. She dumped the bucket then replaced it before stripping off her clothes, dropping everything in the wicker laundry hamper and heading for the shower.

Her nipples felt extra tender as hot water streamed over them. She soaped herself and reminisced about her lover's hands on her body. It was so strange to know him so intimately without having a face to put to her fantasy man.

She knew from touch he possessed a rugged, athletic body, a little on the hairy side. She remembered his height from the Mardi Gras masked ball; he was tall, but not enormous. His hair had been very dark. But his face was a blank. Kind of like the criminals they showed on TV with their faces blacked out.

She dressed in old cutoffs and a navy T-shirt then hauled out her cleaning supplies. With all the hours she worked, she should get a cleaning service, but she kind of liked her Saturday morning ritual. Plus, she hated strangers in her place. They might put her belongings in the wrong spot or mess with things they had no business messing with.

Her lips thinned, the furniture polishing cloth in midswirl on her bedside table. That man, whoever he was, had insinuated she was a control freak. She rubbed hard, shining that table like it had never been shined in its existence. Her muscles ached and sweat beaded her forehead when she finally finished.

She was not a control freak. She just liked things orderly. What was wrong with that?

When she fed her fish, she noticed the plants getting a little ragged; a couple had uprooted and floated to the top. She replanted them in the corner where she liked them, then removed a spot of algae that shaded the sparkling glass of the tank.

Control freak. Maybe she'd bring handcuffs with her next time. Then he'd see a control freak.

As warmth rushed through her body, she decided to phone the hotel right away and book the same room.

Never a woman to put things off, especially not something she really wanted to do, she grabbed the phone book, found the number for the Shaftsbury and dialed. While it rang, she pictured the lobby as it had appeared the night before, empty and echoing with her footsteps. She had a brief vision of her unknown lover traversing the same lobby some time ahead of her, and she had that disconcerting vision of height, strength, dark hair and the blacked-out face.

She shivered with remembered pleasure and the absurdity of what she was doing. It was almost a relief when a female voice answered the phone, effectively shutting off the video playing in her head. "Yes," Genna said, "I'd like to book a room for next Friday night, room 1604."

"One moment, please…"

Genna didn't know why the woman, why anyone, bothered to use such a useless phrase. Invariably it meant she'd wait interminably, listening to tinny music that bore no resemblance to the original composition. Fortunately she was on her cordless phone and could continue her cleaning. She dragged a chair over to the window and climbed up to dust her venetian blinds.

The woman's voice came back on. "Sorry, ma'am, that room's already booked. I could give you another."

"No! It has to be 1604. It just has to." For the first time she regretted that she had no way to contact her mystery lover. She could see herself next Friday skulking outside someone else's hotel room, asking every strange man who came near if he was Neptune. She'd be thrown out on her brainless butt.

"Sorry, Ma'am. That room is already booked next Friday."

"Couldn't you move that party to a different room?

It's very important I have 1604. I'm, uh, very super-stitious.''

''So's the gentleman who booked it a quarter of an hour ago. He stipulated that room.''

''A quarter of an hour...'' Understanding dawned, and with it a spurt of irritation. Of all the high-handed, chauvinistic... She'd told him *she'd* book the room for next week. She'd written it in her note. Well, two could play at being high-handed. ''What about the following Friday?''

''One moment please.''

Perry Como crooned in her ear for about thirty seconds. ''No. The room's booked then, too.''

''By the same party?'' Genna asked through clenched teeth.

''I'm afraid I can't give out that information.''

''When might that particular room be free on a Friday night?''

''One moment please.''

Her blinds snapped and popped as she dusted them ruthlessly, muttering violent oaths while schmaltzy music played in her head.

''Ma'am, that room would be available in January of next year.''

She gasped at the outright gall of the man. No one but Neptune could be so arrogant. She'd have to think up a special punishment for her sea god cum prince. ''Thank you.''

''Did you want me to take a booking?''

''No, thank you.''

She hopped off the chair and replaced the phone with such mildness she marveled at her own control.

Obviously, Neptune had made the permanent booking.

She had to admit it made sense that he'd booked the room for months ahead so as to ensure it was available to them every Friday. But the utter, unmitigated arrogance of the gesture took Genna's breath away.

Was she no more than a call girl? An arranged affair that could be booked into one's electronic organizer with a couple of keystrokes? Part of Genna's brain admired the simple efficiency of the move, even as the woman in her took offense at the way he'd been so sure of her compliance.

"Egotistical bast—" Her door buzzer interrupted her rant. She glanced at the clock from habit, not because she was expecting anyone.

Maybe it was Nick, come to fix her leaky faucet.

She got a funny pang in her stomach as she crossed to her intercom. She still felt strange about the way they'd ended their conversation in his office. He'd made her think about things she didn't want to think about. She wasn't sure she wanted to face him again so soon. Still, her faucet did need fixing.

She pushed the intercom button. "Yes?"

"It's Marcy."

"Come on up," she said, wondering what Marcy was doing here. They didn't live within dropping-in vicinity, and besides, they'd just seen each other last night.

It didn't take long to find out what her best friend wanted.

"Okay, spill," Marcy said as soon as she was inside, two take-out lattes in her hands and a bag of bagels under one arm. Her hair was still damp from the shower, and there was a faded red in her cheeks from prolonged exertion.

Genna blinked. "Did you win your squash game?"

Marcy grinned with evil delight. "I demolished her. I'm now number three on the women's squash ladder. I'm aiming to hit the top spot before the end of the year."

"Wow." Sometimes she forgot that Marcy was as ambitious as she. No wonder they managed to remain such good friends; they were a lot alike.

"Now it's your turn to talk. I'll get the truth out of you if I have to beat it out."

When her friend turned all that energy and focus her way, Genna knew it was hopeless to try and hold out. Another trait they had in common was stubborn determination. She picked up a latte, knowing they'd be the same: two tall skinnies with no sugar.

She grabbed plates, knives, cream cheese and napkins and placed them on the granite breakfast bar that separated the kitchen from the living area. When they were both settled, she gulped her coffee as though it were brandy, and might give her false courage.

All she got was a scorched tongue.

"Well?" Marcy prompted, her eyes trained on Genna like twin scalpels ready to slice away excuses or hedging.

"I met a guy," she said at last, giving in to the inevitable.

"Met a guy as in I'm-having-the-greatest-sex-of-my-life? Or as in possibly-have-a-date-for-the-first-time-this-millennium?"

"The first one," Genna said, deciding not to quibble about the other part. She must have had at least three dates since the dawn of the new millennium, just so she could show up at office functions with a respectable male. She didn't want people thinking she was a total loser who couldn't get a date.

"Ooh, I knew it." Marcy grinned with nosy delight. "You know, the only reason I kept you as a friend after I married Darren was so I could have an exciting, vicarious sex life. I have to tell you you've been a real disappointment. Until now." She rustled into the bag and drew out a bagel, settling back into her seat with undisguised glee.

"Do you want that toasted?" Genna half-rose.

"Sit!" Marcy commanded, chomping into her bagel, the twin scalpels turned her way once more. "And spill," she mumbled with her mouth full.

"You're not going to like it."

"You're having great sex. What's not to like?" She narrowed her eyes doubtfully. "It is great sex, right?"

The grin came from the deepest part of Genna's womanhood and spread to her lips. "The best," she whispered, unable to prevent a slight blush.

A cackle of glee greeted her admission. "So, who is he?"

This was the part Genna had dreaded. She took a napkin and polished a damp coffee ring from the cool gray surface. "I don't know."

Total silence met her admission. She glanced up.

Marcy continued chewing, a stunned look on her face. Several beats passed. "What do you mean, you don't know? Are you shagging a ghost?"

"Not a ghost." A smile curled her lips. "A sea god."

"I think you went without so long your brain dried up. Quit jerking me around. Who is he?"

"This is why I didn't tell you last night at the movie. I'm having sex with a total stranger."

Marcy swallowed and dropped her bagel, her face registering horror. "And I used to think you were the smart one. You're, like, picking guys up in bars or what?"

"No. It's nothing like that. I may know him, but I don't think so. It's just that we've always made love in the dark." She dropped her head to her hands in frustration. "It's impossible to explain. Forget I said anything."

"I've got a big cup of coffee and Darren's not expecting me home until three. You'd better start talking."

A glance at Marcy's worried face was all it took. This woman was like a sister to her; she deserved the truth. And maybe she could help Genna sort out her confused feelings.

She took a deep breath. "Remember the firm retreat I went to in New Orleans?"

Marcy nodded.

"Well, there was this garden..."

It was a relief to finally talk freely about her bizarre liaison. Marcy sat transfixed, her gaze never leaving Genna's face, her bagel forgotten in her lap while Genna told her everything, from the night of the masked ball to the note she'd left the sleeping man just a few hours ago.

When the story ended, Marcy sat for a long time.

"Well? What do you think? Am I certifiable?"

"I think maybe he's the one," her friend said in amazement.

"What one?" Genna felt a flicker of irritation. Ever since Marcy had got married, she seemed convinced Genna should do the same.

"The one who'll convince you there's more to life than work."

Genna shook her head impatiently. "You don't understand."

"Yeah, sweetie, I do. We grew up together, remember? You'd bring home a report card that would be all A's except for one B and you'd get reamed out for not getting straight A's. You've never said, but I've always got the feeling you thought it was your fault when your parents split."

"I really don't think—"

"You're always working to do better, exceed every standard. But real life isn't a scorecard. What mark do you think you'd get in your life right now? Huh? A for career. F for everything else."

That stung. "Well, now I have a sex life. An A-plus sex life," Genna raised her chin, her competitive instincts aroused.

"A fling with a stranger is not a real relationship. Raises your mark to a D tops. But maybe this guy's a step in the right direction. Maybe he'll help you kick back and get a life."

"Why is everybody so interested in my personal life all of a sudden?" Genna wanted to know, feeling her face flush with indignation.

"Define everybody."

"You, Nick, even the guy last night told me some twisted fairy tale about a control-freak princess."

Marcy's laugh was deep and throaty. "Well, Princess Genna, what are you going to do about it?"

Before she could answer, her door buzzer went again.

This time it was Nick. She pushed the button to let him in then glared at Marcy. "What a coincidence. Did he call you?"

"No!" Marcy glared. "I figured out you're totally screwed up all by myself."

They continued to glare at each other for a moment, then Genna dropped her gaze. "I'd be mad at you if you weren't absolutely right. Damn it. What am I doing?"

While she stood by the door waiting for Nick, she realized she didn't want to see him right now. It was all too weird and she was too uncertain of herself. If her two best friends tag-teamed her about this she'd lose it completely.

She raised her head to beg Marcy not to bring up her personal deficiencies in front of Nick but it was too late. He was already tapping on the door.

She opened it and forced a carefree smile on her face.

It wasn't a yuppie lawyer who stood there, it was a working man, complete with a hefty toolbox. "Hi," he said. "Somebody call a plumber?" Even as his words teased, his gaze scrutinized her face as though trying to read her thoughts, and once more her face reddened. When would these two get off her back about her personal life?

She stepped back with a jerk. "Come on in. Join

the party." She let Nick in, watching intently when he spotted Marcy. But he looked naturally surprised to see her. He gave her the grin he kept for his oldest friends. "Hi, Marcy," he said, putting down his tool-box to give her a kiss on the cheek. "How are the kids?"

"They're fine." *Does he know?* she mouthed to Genna as Nick bent for his toolbox.

No! she mouthed back, shaking her head frantically. Nick did not know about her sexual escapades with a stranger and she didn't want him to know. She wasn't sure why, just that she didn't.

He wore ancient jeans and a tatty T-shirt. Still, he managed to look good. He was the kind of guy who'd be just as at home on a construction crew as he was in a boardroom. "Want some coffee?" Genna asked him. "I could put on a pot."

"No, thanks." He squatted and opened the cup-board door under her sink. "You two just go on talking about your wild sex lives, and I'll pretend I can't hear."

Rolling her eyes, as though she and Marcy hadn't been doing just that, she said brightly, "So, Marcy, how did you like that recipe for tuna casserole I gave you?"

Marcy grinned back, raising her voice so Nick wouldn't miss a mendacious word. "It was delicious. Especially when I added the water chestnuts."

"Don't the crushed potato chips on top just make it so special?" she gushed, while she and Marcy made gagging noises to each other.

"I always put extra mayonnaise in mine, makes it so creamy."

"I'll have to remember that. You don't find it too much on top of the canned mushroom soup?"

"Oh, stop. You're making my mouth water," Nick said from the kitchen.

Marcy gagged so artistically she choked and then started laughing. "Hey, Nick. That reminds me. We're having a dinner party next week. Darren has a new public relations director in his company. She's single and new to town. He thinks you two might hit it off."

Nick rose, his shirt straining across his chest muscles, his biceps beautifully defined as he twisted the connection nut off the water supply hose. He flicked a glance at Genna before turning his gaze on Marcy. Genna had the oddest feeling, almost like jealousy, when he said, "Sure. Darren has great taste in women." He winked, and sent Marcy a killer grin that had her blushing. "Not that you have such good taste. You dumped me for him."

Marcy only got more flustered. "That's not exactly... I mean it was both of us..."

Nick chuckled. "Forget about it. You were meant for Darren. I guess I was meant for someone else."

"Maybe Darren's PR lady," Genna said tartly. Here she'd thought the two of them were interested in *her* personal life. But apparently Nick's love life was more interesting.

Another shrug and that enigmatic expression in his eyes. "Who knows?"

"What about me?" Genna interrupted the mutual admiration society. "Aren't I invited to the party?"

"Sure you are."

Her eyes narrowed. "You're not going to set me

up with somebody are you?'' She absolutely hated setups, they were always disastrous. Thanks very much, but she preferred to choose her own men.

''No. Everybody knows you're emotionally unavailable. But we love you, so come anyway. And feel free to bring a date.'' Marcy sent her a challenging glance, which she had to ignore since Nick was standing right there.

''I am not emotionally unavailable. So make sure you put on extra food in case I bring someone.'' She glared back then went to her desk for her Day-Timer. ''When's the party?''

''Next Friday night.''

There was a clang and then a curse as Nick dropped the pipe wrench onto the kitchen floor.

''Friday?'' She flipped a page, feeling dizzy. Of all nights it had to be Friday? That was her night with the stranger. Damn, damn, triple damn. ''Friday. Oh. I…um…I won't be able to stay very late. I have, um…a breakfast meeting Saturday morning.''

Marcy sent her a glance that could be loosely interpreted as, *I know where you're going, and it isn't an early-breakfast meeting.*

7

FLYING TOASTERS.

Genna watched, her head propped on the palm of her left hand and a little smile curving her lips, as silver-winged toasters flapped across her computer screen. They were just so cute. And she bet the one on the left was a girl, and the one flapping like mad behind her was a boy toaster and when they cruised off her screen they'd—

She jerked her head up.

What the hell was she doing having sexual fantasies about her screen saver?

She glared at the phone. It was all his fault. *Mr. Neptune,* undersea god and wrecker of careers. If she could just pick up the phone and call him, just hear his voice, maybe meet for a drink or a movie, perhaps she could get through the day without wandering off into bizarre fantasies about flying toasters.

Which just went to prove that she wasn't emotionally unavailable at all. It was her lover who was unavailable—until Friday night.

She glanced at her Rolex. Tuesday, 3:05 p.m. and seventeen point two seconds. She wished for once it wasn't quite so accurate, since she was practically counting her days by the millisecond.

Would Friday never come?

Her body, which until now had dutifully done its job without any excess demands, had turned into a ravenous sex beast. She had never felt so aware of her body, of the way it moved, and how it reacted to different sensations.

It was as though she'd been frozen and now she was beginning to thaw. She found herself inhaling the aromas at the fruit and vegetable market, noting the different spices and textures on her tongue as she tasted her food. This morning she'd wasted at least a minute pausing to enjoy the sensation when she rubbed moisturizer into her skin.

Strange indeed to be challenged by sensory overload at the law offices of Donne, Green and Raddison. But even here she noticed the rich aroma of coffee when she entered the coffee room. Stopped to smell the standard arrangement of flowers in the reception area. She'd almost laughed at herself as she realized she'd literally stopped to smell the roses.

She shook her head and pulled up the file she was working on.

"Ah, Genna."

She glanced up to find Maureen in her doorway, holding a paper.

"Hi. What's up?"

"It's about this memo."

"The building with the broken-down heating system that cost our client two days of productivity when the building was closed? What's the problem?"

Maureen grinned at her. "I think we should move our offices there. Imagine having a *climax*-controlled office."

"*Climax*-controlled? I wrote that?" Genna clapped

a hand to her mouth. "I meant climate. Climate-controlled."

Maureen dropped the memo on her desk. "Talk about your Freudian slip."

"Thanks for catching that," she said weakly. Oh, Lord, she was seeing sex everywhere.

She'd never thought of herself as particularly imaginative, but these days she felt she could write her own version of the *Kama Sutra*. With detailed drawings.

Shaking her head, as though she could rattle her brains back into some semblance of order, she grabbed a notebook and headed for Nick's office for an update on the Ross case. Maybe a good reminder of how miserable love could turn would get her brain unscrambled.

She hurtled out of her doorway only to bash into a warm, muscular chest. Her breasts struck first, making her suck in her breath sharply, as sensation shot through her.

Two hands, warm and steady grabbed her arms. She glanced up to see Nick staring down at her, dragging air into his own lungs.

"You okay?" he asked.

"Apart from going down a bra size, I think I'm fine," she gasped, but her voice was kind of breathless as she found herself staring at the contours of his chest through the crisp white shirt. "And, I may have creased your shirt."

Still he held her, and the heat traveling from his fingers into her upper arms was amazing. Being so near him, she could smell the starch in his professionally laundered shirt, see his chest rise and fall as he breathed, feel some kind of current that felt...well, like attraction. Oh, man. She was really losing it. Now she was even projecting her sexual longing onto Nick. She glanced up, startled to find him gazing at her, a crease forming between his brows.

"Are you sure you're all right?"

"Yes." Nerves made her laugh as she stepped back. She was absolutely fine except that she was going crazy. Was she turning into some kind of nymphomaniac all of a sudden, that she should find herself thinking sexy thoughts about her only male friend? "I was on my way to see you."

"And I was on my way to see you." He grinned at her, and the pulse that had just started to settle took to hammering again. How many women had she watched fall under the spell of that charming grin? It had never affected her before. Why now?

"I guess we might as well meet in your office," he said, "It's closer."

"Yes. Right. Sure." She backed through her office door and collapsed into her chair.

He sat opposite and she wondered if he'd felt it, too, that surprising zing of attraction. If so, he didn't show it. "We have a problem with the Ross case," he said without preamble.

All thoughts of sex fled as she took in his words.

She hated this. There were three little kids in the photograph Tiffany Ross had shown them. She didn't want the Ross family to break up. She kind of liked Tiffany, even if she wasn't the sharpest knife in the drawer. "What's the problem?" She straightened her notebook and prepared to take notes.

"I talked to Mr. Ross's lawyer today and explained

our client's position—that she hasn't committed adultery and would like to work things out.''

Genna nodded. It was the first duty of the lawyers in a divorce case to explore the possibility of a reconciliation. ''And?''

''They have a private investigator's report that allegedly proves she had an affair.''

Genna frowned. ''But she seemed so sincere when she told us she hadn't slept with that actor fellow. What would a private investigator have seen?'' She closed her eyes and replayed Tiffany's story in her head.

''Maybe she played doctor with 'Ersatz' more than she admitted to us,'' Nick suggested.

Still frowning, she pulled up the file of her typed notes from the interview and began to scroll. ''She admits to meeting him for coffee, and lunch.'' She glanced up. ''That would have looked pretty cozy.''

''But not cozy enough to be proof of adultery.''

She kept scrolling, and then her heart sank. ''Oh, oh. Look at this.''

He came round the desk and stood at her shoulder, reading from the screen. She tried to concentrate on her work, but Nick was so close she could feel the warmth from his body. He rested a hand on her desk and she noticed the dark hair on his forearm, and the strength in his hand.

He had nice hands. Square and purposeful. Hands that were as at home with a wrench as they were gesturing in defense of a client. And if his romantic career was anything to go on, they'd pleased their share of women in his time. Once more that disconcerting tingle traveled through her body.

"I see what you're getting at," he said, the words sending a current of air to tickle her hair. "Her husband told her he wanted a divorce the day after Mrs. Ross had lunch with the phony doctor. Damn it. She went inside his building just a few minutes after he did. It's easy to draw the conclusion that she was up there having sex with that jerk. That's what's in the report."

Genna nodded, forcing her thoughts back to work. "Yes. And we know she was inside his apartment building for quite a while, searching for his mailbox and reading the newspaper article."

"It's all circumstantial, but damn." Nick straightened and began to pace. "This won't help her save her marriage."

"No. All we have is her word that she didn't sleep with this guy."

"We'll have to find Dr. Ersatz—what was his real name?"

She consulted her notes. "Simon Chance."

"We need him to corroborate her story."

"Oh, that should be fun. I suppose you want me to try to track him down?"

He gently pulled the back of her hair, forcing her to look up at him. Even upside down his face was arresting with those gray eyes and the dark hair. "Is this going to cost me more manual labor?"

She grinned at his upside-down face. "Well, my sink's not leaking anymore. But I'll think of something. We'll call it a blank IOU."

"And I should trust you with a blank IOU because?" He mimicked her earlier challenge.

"You shouldn't. Not at all. Better find somebody else to do your dirty work."

"There is nobody else." He continued gazing down at her and she felt as if things really were upside down. He just didn't seem like the usual Nick. Then he gave her a crooked grin. "I'll do anything but wash windows."

"Too chauvinistic?" she challenged.

"Too scared of heights. Unless you move to the ground floor, windows are out." He tweaked her hair. "Thanks. In the meantime, I'll see if I can get a copy of the P.I.'s report."

She thought about Mrs. Ross going through a whole box of tissues in Nick's office. Sure seemed like she wanted her husband back. "Do you think there's a chance we can save her marriage?"

He'd reached the door, but turned back to answer her soft question. "Well, he filed for divorce right after he got the P.I.'s report. I'm guessing he doesn't have another woman. He's hurt and angry and he thinks his wife was cheating on him." He shrugged. "It all comes down to whether he loves her. You'd be surprised what a man will do for the woman he loves." And with that enigmatic comment, he strode out of her office, leaving Genna staring after him.

"Hi, sweetie, come on in," Marcy said, standing in the doorway of her large apartment.

"Sorry I'm late. I got caught up with something at work." Then she'd rushed home to shower and prepare for later. Her body hummed. Only a few more hours.

After deliberating on what to wear for a dinner with

intimate friends followed by wild sex with an intimate stranger, she'd settled on a black two-piece. A short skirt and camisole top with spaghetti straps. On her feet were black strappy sandals and she had an over-size colorful shawl around her shoulders.

She liked the outfit. It was sexy without being flashy, stretchy so it was easy to yank off, and under it she wore nothing but a thong. And what was hidden under that thong throbbed with anticipation.

As she entered, Genna was conscious of being the last to arrive. The party was in full swing as she greeted Marcy and Darren's friends.

All couples. She knew most of them, and was usually perfectly comfortable to be the only unattached female. She'd just never felt so much like the odd one out.

Nick was here. She noticed his tall form out on the patio, so she wasn't in fact the only single person. Except that he was talking to a petite brunette with a big smile, which gave them the illusion of coupledom, and Genna the feeling of being the only non-couple in the apartment.

"What can I get you to drink, Genna?" her host asked after he'd greeted her with a bear hug. Darren was a lot like a bear, big and cuddly. It always amazed her that Marcy had chosen him over Nick. Nick who was so very good-looking and…well, virile. But there was no doubt that Darren and Marcy were happily married, just as Nick was happily single.

A happily single playboy.

With a new playbunny on the string by the look of things.

While Genna sipped white wine and joined two

couples discussing mortgage rates, she chose a seat that gave her an unobstructed view of Nick and his new friend.

This was obviously the public relations woman Marcy had wanted him to meet. Genna felt certain the woman must be excellent at her job. She appeared warm and friendly, talkative, interesting, and she sure seemed interested in Nick. He had a nod and a wave for Genna the moment he caught sight of her, and then it was back to the fascinating PR woman.

"I'll introduce you," Marcy said on her way by, as she saw the direction of Genna's glance.

"No, that's okay. I don't want to interrupt them. They look so cozy."

Marcy sent her an amused glance. "They do, don't they? I've always thought Nick deserved someone very special."

"After you dumped him, you mean."

Marcy opened her mouth and closed it again. "It wasn't quite that simple." She glanced at Nick and the PR woman. "It would be strange if Nick got married." She contemplated Genna for a long moment. "I imagine it would affect your friendship with him if his wife was the jealous type."

"Nick? Married?" She laughed, even as a bubble of panic rose in her throat. "I can't imagine it. He loves women too much."

"He's also Italian. You know, big families eating plates of spaghetti and drinking red wine. Weddings with three hundred close relatives. Deep down he's a family man—and when he finds the right woman, watch out."

Genna's chest started to feel tight. She'd never

imagined Nick with a wife other than Marcy, and after that didn't work out, she'd never seen him with anyone for longer than a season. As reliably as the crocuses replaced snow, or autumn leaves turned color, Nick changed women.

As she glanced again at Nick and his new friend, she was self-aware enough to recognize that the pang she felt was jealousy. After Nick and Marcy split up, he'd always chosen impossible women, women Genna knew he'd never commit to. But here was a perfectly nice, very commitment-worthy woman.

What if he did settle down? What would it be like not to have him in her life in the way she'd grown accustomed to? Not to be able to call on him when she wanted advice, someone to see a movie with, fix her leaky faucet?

He glanced her way and as their gazes connected it seemed to her that she saw him for the first time. Not as Marcy's almost-husband, not as her friend, but as a man. An attractive, sexy man. A man...

The buzz of conversation dimmed, the background music faded, and she forgot to breathe. A man a woman like Genna could fall for.

If he'd glanced away, the spell would have broken. But he didn't glance away. He held her gaze with his own, and the expression in his gray eyes changed, from curious, to downright smoldering. He took a step forward, toward Genna, and she wondered what she'd do when he reached her. Panic beat at her chest with fluttery wings and she swallowed in a quick nervous gulp.

Then his companion reached up to touch his arm

and Nick gave his head a tiny shake as though to clear it and turned his attention back to the PR woman.

Genna shook her own head even harder, appalled at her own foolishness. She tried to concentrate on the conversation at hand. Denise and Randy, the couple she sat beside, were still talking about real estate. Not real-estate law as she'd immediately assumed, but buying a house.

She was about to ask what was wrong with their centrally located apartment when she saw Randy's hand stray to Denise's belly in an unconscious gesture. As his hand pulled the material of her cotton sundress tight, the bulge of pregnancy became apparent. As did the reason for the move to the suburbs.

Possessive husbands, babies, suburbs; she tried to summon her usual horror at the grim trio but for the first time, marriage, a newborn and suburbia didn't sound all that awful. Maybe there was even a tiny bit of appeal at the obvious closeness between husband and wife. In having a child together, worrying about mortgage rates.

She sighed, and rose to help Marcy in the kitchen.

"WOULD YOU QUIT looking at your watch? You're making me nervous," Marcy said.

"Oh, sorry. I just..." Heat burned her face as she slapped butter and salad dressing on Marcy's antique oak table where the buffet dinner was set up.

"You just can't wait to blow this joint and get your rocks off. I know. But you don't have to look so darned eager about it."

"You're just jealous," Genna announced smugly.

"Damn right. Just watching you, you've got me so

twitchy I can't wait to ditch my guests so I can jump Darren's bones. With the kids sleeping over at my mother's, we'll have the whole place to ourselves.''

Genna giggled, feeling excitement trickle through her entire body. ''Isn't it great? Knowing we have something like this to look forward to?''

''Something like what to look forward to?'' Nick asked from behind her, reaching around her to grab a carrot stick off the crudités plate.

Genna felt her face heat, and refused to turn around.

Marcy winked at him over Genna's shoulder. ''That was girl talk.''

''My favorite kind,'' he said with teasing humor.

''I'll get the bread,'' Genna gasped, feeling the warmth of his body behind her, hearing Marcy's voice without a clue what she was saying. Rapidly, she escaped to the kitchen.

NICK HAD a pretty good feeling he knew exactly what Genna was looking forward to. And she couldn't be anticipating her Friday night of passion any more than he was.

Her legs appeared long and sexy in the short skirt and strappy shoes. And the contours of her breasts were so natural he had a feeling she wasn't wearing a bra. His hands tingled, realizing he'd soon be finding out just exactly what she wasn't wearing under her outfit.

Her makeup was a little heavier than he was used to. He liked it. It gave her a dramatic look. Her eyes appeared huge, her lips glossy red like succulent fruit, begging to be tasted.

He knew just the man for the job.

There was something else about her tonight, too. Her body was relaxed, her posture open. And she was putting out some kind of sizzling energy. He'd felt it when their gazes caught and held earlier. When he'd seen the awareness in her eyes.

He'd been so lured by her new but unmistakable awareness of him as a man, he'd almost walked right off on Kathy, Darren's new public relations officer. Fortunately she'd put her hand on his arm and called him back to reality before he had time to follow his impulse to walk over to Genna, hoist her over his shoulder and keep on going.

He didn't plan to keep her hostage forever. He figured fifty years or so ought to do it.

He grinned to himself as she finally emerged from the kitchen, refusing to catch his eye, still a little red-faced. Good. He liked her flushed and off-kilter. It made her more human, and a lot more fun.

"Okay, everybody." Marcy clapped her hands for attention. "Dinner's on the table. Fill a plate and find a spot to sit." Then her gaze scanned the room and her hands flapped in annoyance. "Where's Darren?"

"I think I saw him head to the bathroom," Genna answered.

"Anything I can do to help?" Nick asked.

"Why does my husband always disappear when I need him?"

"Self-preservation?"

She grinned at him, this woman who was a great friend, but never meant to be his wife. "Count yourself lucky. You can pour the wine."

As he did, people filled their plates and settled on

living room couches, oak dining chairs and outdoor patio furniture.

Genna, still helping with the food, was one of the last to sit, perching on the slate hearth. Nick shoved food on a plate and grabbed himself a glass of merlot then headed her way.

Only to be cut off by Darren's business partner, Keith the letch. The man wasn't yet forty and already on his third marriage. Nick narrowed his eyes as Keith did his best to look up Genna's skirt while settling himself beside her.

Nick clenched his teeth and turned away, finding that everyone had left the second seat of a loveseat empty beside Kathy. Doing his best to look delighted, he took his seat beside her. And spent the rest of the evening talking about God-knows-what while keeping narrowed eyes on Keith the letch flirting with Genna, whose skirt kept riding higher.

Along with his own blood pressure.

She was his, damn it. Why was it that no one knew it but him?

The one good thing was, he didn't have to bother keeping track of the time. Genna did it for him. With pure masculine enjoyment, he noted how often she looked at her watch, knowing just what was on her mind.

He felt his own excitement build each time he watched her glance surreptitiously at the elegant gold watch on her slim wrist.

When her lips parted and she touched a hand to her chest, he knew it was time. Instinctively his body tightened.

She rose gracefully, her cheeks delicately flushed,

eyes sparkling and made her way to Marcy. He couldn't hear what the two women said, but there was stifled giggling and a quick hug and then Genna was out the door.

He glanced at his own watch. It was going to be tight, getting to the hotel ahead of Genna, but he was counting on his knowledge of her. If he knew Genna, she'd stop at her place first to freshen up and brush her teeth. Which would give him just enough time.

He swapped business cards with Kathy, knowing he'd never call her, and left her in the clutches of Keith the letch.

He gave Genna five minutes head start, then waited until Marcy was deep in conversation. Women were just too damned intuitive about some things. He preferred to make his excuses to Darren, definitely the denser of the two.

Once he'd sauntered out the door, he did the hundred-yard dash at Olympic record speed, jumped in his car and roared off.

He entered the hotel lobby at eight minutes to eleven and fished out the key card, glad he'd checked in earlier. He hoped his hot date didn't arrive early, tonight of all nights.

He sprinted across the lobby and punched the elevator button.

"Come on, come on," he muttered. Jabbing it again, he glanced toward the Shaftsbury's main entrance, ready to bolt round a corner if he spotted Genna.

Finally the elevator arrived with a ping and he breathed a sigh of relief as it lifted him with silent speed to the sixteenth floor.

He raced down the corridor, key in hand, and was inside the room within seconds, before blowing out a breath.

Still five to eleven. He dashed into the bathroom, yanking his shirt over his head as did. He pulled his pants off with one hand, turning the shower on with the other. In, shampoo, quick soap, out. He grabbed a towel with one hand and his toothbrush with the other.

Two minutes to eleven. He shrugged into the hotel robe, sticking a couple of condoms into the pocket and taking another handful to put on the bedside table, then packed his stuff into his overnighter. Then he flicked off the lights and settled down to wait.

Except he couldn't settle.

He was wired with excitement at what would happen during the hours ahead. The whole dinner had been a kind of foreplay, with Genna in her short skirt and flirty shoes, her blue eyes telegraphing messages she'd never sent his way before. He was no psychiatrist, but he wondered if, on some level, she knew perfectly well whom she was sleeping with on Fridays.

He wanted badly to believe this newfound awareness was connected with their affair. She was changing, whether she wanted to admit it or not.

Sleeping beauty was slowly waking.

GENNA'S HEART TREMBLED.

Her whole body trembled inside and out as she knocked quietly on the door of room 1604. She'd driven around the block three times, determined not to be too eager. Five after eleven seemed like a good time to knock. Not too keen, but not so late as to be rude.

The door opened and her mouth went dry. All evening she'd been longing for this moment. Now it was here.

Slowly, she entered the darkness.

The door shut behind her and she jumped as hands came out of nowhere to touch her shoulders. She dropped her purse at her feet and moved into his arms even as he pushed her back against the door.

"I'm so hungry for you," he whispered.

She could do nothing but whimper as he kissed her with all the passion and urgency she felt.

His tongue invaded her mouth, taking possession with fiery hunger and she grabbed the back of his head, clutching damp tufts as she pulled him closer. She was on fire for him, desperate to take and be taken.

If he tried to tease her or torment her tonight, she thought she'd die.

But there was no waiting, no teasing. His urgency was as keen, his haste as evident as he reached for her top and peeled it over her head.

The door felt cool and hard at her back as his hands clutched her breasts, squeezing and rubbing until she moaned.

She yanked at the belt on his robe, then opened the garment and pushed it off his shoulders. His hands left her for a moment and she heard rustling, then the robe brushed past her on its way to the floor.

He was naked.

And she needed to be, too. She reached under her skirt and hauled her panties off in a fever of need even as she felt him sheath himself. Then he shoved her skirt up, and took her against the door, driving deep and high so she felt him strike the very head of her womb.

She sobbed noisily as she came, suddenly and violently. She wanted to cry out his name, but she didn't know what it was.

Instead she cried, "Yes, oh, darling. Yes."

He plunged wildly once more and then she felt his whole body shudder. His lips were buried in her neck at the time so she couldn't be certain, but she thought he called out her name.

They were wilder than they'd ever been, taking of each other as though they couldn't get enough. And yet, as she slipped out in the small hours of the morning, she felt vaguely dissatisfied.

It was great sex, but it was only sex.

She wanted more.

8

GENNA WALTZED into Nick's office late Monday morning, waving an Internet printout like a victory banner. "Ha!" she said. "I've got him!"

"Dr. Ersatz?" With a warm smile, Nick glanced up from the document he was reading. His expression more than warm, really.

She swallowed and dropped her gaze to the printout. "In the flesh. Appearing in *Romeo and Juliet* of all things at someplace called the Alternative Works Theaterspace. I think I'll enjoy watching him die at the end."

"You're going to see the play?" Nick sounded surprised.

"Not me. Us. You and me. It's in a grungy area near the strip. I'd be scared without a big strong bodyguard." She pointed at him. "That would be you. Besides, I figure you can intimidate him a little when we interview him together."

He didn't look thrilled about being recruited to play bad cop to her good cop. "I haven't read *Romeo and Juliet* since high school. And I thought it sucked."

"Well, when I phoned for tickets, the woman called it 'the new *Romeo and Juliet*.' Maybe they've added space aliens or something for the culturally inept." She grinned. "You'll feel right at home."

"You couldn't make this simple and just call him at his apartment?" As usual, Nick's sleeves were rolled, but today he'd also loosened his tie and the first button of his shirt. A little dark chest hair showed, making her think suddenly of her secret lover and the way he made her shiver when he rubbed his hairy chest against her naked breasts. Mmm. It was also easier to look at Nick's forearms and his chest than it was to gaze into his eyes.

She felt suddenly wary around him. That bizarre moment at Marcy's dinner, when their eyes had locked, kept coming back to her at odd moments. She had to stop thinking about it. Nick was her friend. She liked him that way.

She dropped her gaze to the Internet printout as she answered his question. "I tried that, obviously. He doesn't have an answering machine, and the one time he picked up the phone and I introduced myself he pretended he wasn't Simon Chance. Said he'd give him a message."

"You told him about Tiffany?"

She glanced up at him. "No. I just said I was a lawyer with Donne, Green and Raddison, and he interrupted and said Simon Chance wasn't home. Then he hung up."

Nick leaned back in his chair. "*Romeo and Juliet,* huh?"

"That's right." She dropped the printout on his desk and walked to the door. Just before she left she turned and grinned. "'Parting is such sweet sorrow, That I shall say good night till it be morrow.'"

THEATER WAS A rather grand word for the sunken pit in which Genna and Nick found themselves. There were no more than a hundred seats of the folding chair guaranteed-to-produce-acute-backache-within-an-hour variety, surrounding a small stage. The theater smelled of dust and infrequently washed bodies.

Their fellow theatergoers were an eclectic mix. Of all ages, they seemed like mostly ex-hippies, retro-hippies and grunge types. Since she and Nick had come straight from work, they stuck out like two very sore thumbs in their business attire.

Genna heard a quiet moan and felt her eyes widen as she noted a couple two rows ahead, their open mouths hungrily devouring each other. The man's hand was under the woman's striped robe, and from the way she was pumping her hips, it was pretty clear what that hand was doing.

"Looks like the show started early," Nick murmured in her ear, causing her to stifle a giggle.

Nick's hand rested lightly on the fake wood arm of his chair and she found herself wondering what it would feel like...

She jerked her attention to the empty stage, hoping like hell he wasn't a mind reader on the side.

Thinking of Nick and her and sex gave her a weird feeling in the pit of her stomach, almost like fear. Ever since that odd moment last Friday when they'd gazed at each other, she was having these uncomfortable feelings. Feelings she didn't want or need. Her life was complicated enough.

The already dim lighting darkened and a single spotlight illuminated the stage.

From out of the darkness boomed an actor's voice.

" 'Two households, both alike in dignity, In fair Verona, where we lay our scene...' '' She settled back, trying to find a comfortable position on the rickety chair. This was Shakespeare. She could abandon herself to a tale of ancient, tragic love and forget about sex for a couple of hours. She needed the break.

The first actor entered the stage to stand under the single spotlight as the prologue continued.

Her breath caught and her eyes bugged open. Was her sex-obsessed mind playing tricks on her? She blinked and looked again.

The man was buck naked.

And so was the next. Soon the stage was crowded with naked bodies while Genna sat there, rigid with shock.

Nick leaned closer, his voice teasing. "When the woman called this the new *Romeo and Juliet,* could you have misheard? This seems to be the nude *Romeo and Juliet.*"

"Oh, my God." She dropped her head in her hands. Trust her to bring Nick to the *nude Romeo and Juliet.* "I'm sorry."

"Don't be. It's better than space aliens. I'm kind of looking forward to seeing Juliet." His deep voice rumbled in her ear, quivering on the edge of a laugh.

She didn't find this at all humorous. "Which one do you think is Simon Chance?"

"I'm guessing he's the nude Romeo."

Genna nodded. She'd come to the same conclusion. He had all the attributes of a successful gigolo. He was blond, handsome, tall and his male equipment was certainly impressive.

She watched for a while, keeping her gaze fixed

above his waist as much as possible and decided he wasn't a bad actor.

Juliet bounced on stage, quite literally, and Genna concluded that the mature course of action was to ignore the fact that the actors were starkers and enjoy the play. It was Shakespeare, after all.

This strategy worked fine until the wedding night scene. Where the nude Romeo and Juliet version cut much of the original play, they were dragging out the wedding night for all it was worth.

The nude Juliet wasn't in the first blush of youth, but she certainly was enthusiastic about her wedding night with Romeo. One glance told Genna Romeo was definitely up for the event.

As they rolled around the stage kissing and…oh, Lord. She refused to cover her eyes. Instead she let her gaze travel around the small theater. There was movement in some of the seats. And all the moaning and sighing wasn't coming from the stage.

"I'm so sorry. This is practically an orgy," she hissed to her partner.

"In iambic pentameter. Amazing."

She had never felt so embarrassed in her life. And yet, even in the sleazy surroundings, watching a Shakespearean peep show, Genna found herself growing warm, very conscious of the man beside her. She heard him breathing, felt his warmth. When her arm accidentally brushed his, she almost gasped aloud at the heat that arced through her body.

She crossed her legs, wishing she'd come to this thing alone. Or with Marcy, which would have been a gigglefest. Or better still, she wished she hadn't come at all.

Beside her, Nick was rigidly still. He must be as mortified as she was. She refused to glance at him and find out.

At least there was no intermission. She couldn't have struggled through chitchat for fifteen minutes. She would have simply abandoned her quest and found another way to contact Simon Chance. Mercifully, the play carried on without a break. The bridal bed, after being heavily romped upon, soon became the death bower where the naked lovers sprawled.

"And to think I used to think Shakespeare was boring," Nick said after the sparse clapping died away.

"Not one word. Not one single word from you," Genna warned, her face flaming once more.

He chuckled with devilish enjoyment. "Let's go backstage before they get dressed and leave."

"Where do you suppose the stage door is?"

"I say we follow where nude Romeo went— through there." And, taking her hand, he pulled her onto the stage and into the wings. They found themselves in dusty darkness. A single dim bulb hung by a wire over a black-carpeted stairway and Nick led her down, still holding her hand. His grasp felt warm and strong and, well, sexy.

She pulled her hand away as soon as they got to the bottom of the stairs.

They emerged into a small dark hallway and followed the muffled sound of voices to a room near the end.

"The undressing room, I presume," Nick said.

She sent him a shut-up glance and knocked on the closed door.

It opened a few inches. "Yeah?" It was nude Mercutio, no longer nude. He looked like a college kid in a ripped T-shirt and scruffy jeans, a few pimples on his imperfectly shaved chin.

"We're looking for Simon Chance," Genna said.

The face disappeared. "Hey, Si. Somebody to see you."

She heard a low voice in reply and then nude Mercutio again. "I don't know. Looks like social workers or cops or somethin'."

More mumbling.

"Nuh-ah. Tell 'em yourself."

Then nude Romeo peered at them from the partially open door, his eyes suspicious slits. He wore a not-quite-white muscle shirt and low slung jeans.

"Simon Chance?"

"What do you want?"

"We saw the show, you were great," she said with a smile she hoped would disarm the suspicion staring at her.

"Yeah? Thanks," he said, and tried to shut the door.

Nick shoved his foot between the door and the jamb. "We also want to talk to you."

"I'm busy."

"It's about a friend of yours. Dr. Ersatz."

The head jerked and the eyes slanted into a nervous glance. "Don't know the dude." Once more he tried to shut the door on them.

Once more Nick's foot blocked the way. "Maybe Juliet knows Dr. Ersatz. We'll ask her."

Genna was puzzled by the Nick's statement, but it made nude Romeo jump. Simon Chance's pale blue eyes widened in obvious panic. "I told you I don't know him. She won't, either. Now beat it."

"Look, Simon. You can spend a few minutes talking to us or I'll tell your new lady about your scam to get lonely ladies in bed. Your choice."

Simon Chance stood there for a moment staring at them.

"Simon, honey, what is it?" Genna recognized the female voice as Juliet's.

"Well?" Nick pressed.

Simon Chance turned and said, "It's some people from the newspaper. They want to do an interview with me. I'll be back in a half hour." He disappeared from the door. Genna heard a loud kiss, then he was back with a battered pack of Marlboros. He jerked his head at them and strode down the corridor, opening another door and motioning them inside.

Genna entered first. It was a small office with a cheap metal desk taking up most of the space desk against the far wall. Newspapers and paper coffee cups were strewn over the surface. An old black dial phone and an ancient computer sat in the midst of the clutter.

There was a cracked vinyl chair and four folding chairs, identical to the theater seats in a rough semicircle. Posters and newspaper clippings hung haphazardly on the dirty beige walls.

Simon shut the door and leaned against it. Somebody must have once told him he looked like Brad Pitt, Genna mused. And he'd cultivated the image to the max. He had shaggy blond hair that she suspected wasn't entirely natural, blue eyes and a boyishly handsome face.

He was also a marriage wrecker and a user of lonely women.

"We're lawyers representing Tiffany Ross and we need your help," Nick said calmly.

"I don't know—"

"Save it. You've got a good thing going here. You don't want to blow it. That Juliet, I bet she looks after you very nicely. On and offstage."

Genna stared at Nick. Was he making this stuff up? It seemed his hunch was right, though. Simon slumped against the door. "What do you want?"

After that it was easy. Genna produced the affidavit she'd already drawn up, which stated Simon had never had sexual intercourse with Tiffany Ross, and further, that she'd never been inside his apartment.

He read it over and she handed him a pen. Not the gold one from her dad, but a cheap ballpoint. "Sign at the bottom if it's true."

"Yeah, it's true." The actor clicked the pen a few times. "What's in this for me?"

"The knowledge that you're saving a marriage," she said.

"Look, I got expenses. Lots of expenses. I figure I'm doing this lady a favor. There should be some consideration."

Nick opened the door and strode out without a word.

"Where's he going? Is he going to bother Juliet?" He glanced around, then darted after Nick. "Hey, dude. Come back here. I'm just signing this thing." He paused just before he put pen to paper. "I won't have to go to court, will I?"

"Shouldn't have to," Nick answered from the doorway.

The young man scrawled his name then tossed the pen onto the metal desk. "There. Can I go now?"

"Thank you, Mr. Chance," Genna said. She picked up the affidavit and replaced it in her portfolio. She left the pen on the desk.

Once they were outside, Genna breathed deeply, glad to get the dank, dusty smell out of her lungs. "How did you know?" she demanded as soon as they were in Nick's car.

"You mean that nude Juliet was his sugar mama?"

"Mmm-hmm."

"I checked out the poster. She's the producer and director. She's probably footing the bill for the show, and I got to thinking she might be footing a lot of Simon's bills." He shrugged. "It was just a hunch."

"Male intuition?" she teased.

"Make fun of it if you must," he said as he pulled into traffic.

She smiled at him. "You did good." They chatted about Tiffany Ross and the case as he drove Genna home, both of them staying away from discussing the play. He smirked once or twice but, to his credit, Nick never mentioned the "new *Romeo and Juliet*" once.

He pulled up outside her building. She got out of the car and so did he.

"What are you doing?" She turned to him, surprised.

"I'm walking you to your door. According to my grandma, that's what gentlemen do."

She glanced at him warily. "Thanks."

"Would you like to go out for dinner?"

She checked her watch. "It's almost midnight. I ate earlier. In fact, so did you."

"I didn't mean tonight. I meant Saturday."

She stared at him, partly in confusion, partly in heart-pounding anticipation. "You need a date for something?"

He sighed. "For somebody so smart, you can be incredibly dense sometimes. I mean like a real date. You and me."

She said the first thing that bounced into her mind. "You only date impossible women."

"Right." A badly suppressed grin kicked up one side of his mouth.

Her jaw dropped in outrage. "I am not impossible."

"High-maintenance is a better term."

"Oh—I—" She sputtered in outrage.

He was openly grinning now, but there was a serious light in his eyes. "So, will you?"

"Go on a date with you." She gazed up at him and thought of how much she wanted to and how scared she was. Being friends was uncomplicated, dating anything but. "I don't know. We've been friends so long, what if we screw it up?"

"It's just dinner. I'm not asking you to pick wedding china."

She thought about spending an evening with him and then felt her eyes narrow as one aspect of the "date" struck her. "What about the good-night kiss?"

"Huh?"

"Is there going to be a good-night kiss? After this date?"

He appeared to give the matter some thought. "That depends on how you shape up as a date."

"Well, assuming I pass the rigorous going-out-with-Nick-Cavallo test and manage to prove by the end of the evening that I am one or all of the following—bulimic, psychotic, father-fixated, lawyer-fixated or dumber than dirt."

"Then I'd say your chances of an end-of-date snog were pretty good."

For all her flip joking, there was a core of fear under her words. Changing their relationship could screw it up completely. What if she disappointed him as a date? What if it killed their friendship? "I don't know. It feels weird. The whole kiss thing. What if it gets blown out of proportion? What if we get performance anxiety?"

"About kissing?"

"It could happen. We could be terrible kissers, our teeth could bump, noses crash into each other. It could be a—"

Her words were cut off with a tiny mew as he stepped forward, pulled her into his arms and covered her lips with his.

Warm and firm, sexy and sweet, his lips hinted at so much. Just as she got over the shock that she was kissing Nick, and started to melt, she wasn't kissing him anymore. He pulled away, leaving her shaken and even more confused.

"What was that for?" she asked in a voice that didn't sound like hers.

"Did our noses bump?"

"No."

"Teeth mash?"

"No." But then they hadn't done the openmouthed thing, so it wasn't a fair question.

"Did you like it?"

"I didn't hate it."

"So, that's the kiss out of the way. I'll pick you up Saturday at eight."

And he strode off, leaving her staring after him.

9

"Am I a slut?" Genna wailed to Marcy after a squash game that left her whole body feeling bruised and rubbery.

Laughter shook Marcy's shoulders. "Sweetie, you have more in common with a nun."

She uncapped her water bottle and chugged half of it down. "I'm just so confused. I'm sleeping with Neptune on Friday, then having a date with Nick on Saturday. Isn't that kind of slutty?"

There was a certain smug expression on her friend's face that made Genna want to smack her. "It might be if you sleep with Nick on Saturday, but based on the way you've been freaking out over one little kiss, I don't think that's going to happen."

Water dribbled down Genna's chin as her mouth dropped open midswallow. "Of course I'm not going to sleep with Nick. I mean…" Her sneakers squeaked as she slumped against the wall outside the squash court. The corridor smelled of rubber and sweat and from inside the next court came the dull, rhythmic thud of the ball and the occasional smack of a racquet hitting a wall.

"Oh, Marcy. I don't know what I'm doing."

Her friend had one leg doubled behind her in a quad stretch. "Do you want to sleep with Nick?"

"No!"

"Why not? He's fantastic in bed."

More water slurped down her chin. "This!" she hissed frantically, flapping her hand between her and Marcy. "This is the reason. I can't sleep with a guy my best friend's slept with. One she almost married."

"Why not? I don't care. And he obviously doesn't care." Marcy switched legs and leaned into the wall for a deeper stretch. "I found my perfect mate, but Nick's still looking. You're still looking—well you're not looking, but you should be."

"But Nick's my friend."

"Darren's my friend. Believe me, liking each other makes the sex way better."

"Would you just shut up about the sex?"

"Look, if that's all that's bothering you—"

"It's not all that's bothering me. I mean, it's a big thing, but, oh, hell. I'm already sleeping with someone."

"The mysterious sex buddy. Right."

"Don't call him that."

"What would you suggest I call him?" Marcy asked with deceptive sweetness. "You don't know his damn name."

"There's something there. Between us. I can't explain it. It's like I want to stop, but I can't."

"Genna, are we having a *9¹/₂ Weeks* obsession going here?" Both feet back on the ground, her friend appeared truly worried. "Trust you to be the only person in the world who can't have a fling. You have to turn it into something deadly serious."

Genna scuffed at the shiny wood floor with her sneaker. "I'm having…feelings about him."

"About a guy you've never seen whose name you don't know?"

It sounded crazy. She was perfectly well aware of that. It was crazy. But Genna had never been a person who ran from the truth. Keeping her eyes on the ground she murmured, "Yes."

"Then, if you're going to kill any chance of going out with Nick over this stranger, you'd better find out who he is. You may have different feelings when you see him in the light."

"You're right. I know you're right. I have to find out who he is."

But she didn't want to. Somehow, she felt sure nothing but complication could arise from bringing her secret fling into the light. Was she the only woman who could fall in love with a total stranger she'd been intimate with?

Had she just failed Casual Sex 101?

MARCY WAS RIGHT, she admitted to herself later as she tossed in bed, physically tired from the grueling squash match but mentally too perturbed for sleep; she couldn't throw away her relationship with Nick because she had feelings for a stranger.

It simply wasn't logical. And Genna was always logical.

She considered the past few weeks. Well, almost always logical.

Nick. When had her feelings for him warmed? When had his feelings for her? She turned and punched her pillow. And why now of all times?

Whatever Marcy said, Genna had her own code of conduct. It wouldn't be right to sleep with one man on Friday night and date another on Saturday. She just wouldn't go to the hotel tomorrow. She'd phone and leave a message canceling their appointment. Then she wouldn't have this icky feeling about dating Nick on Saturday after spending the night with Neptune on Friday.

Having made that decision, and feeling pretty damn virtuous about it, she fell asleep.

The next morning she got through her getting-ready-for-work routine in record time. She glanced at the phone as she was leaving, but decided she could call the hotel just as easily from the office.

Once settled at her desk, it was a simple matter to pick up the phone. But it was impossible to make the call to the hotel. Every time she tried to cancel, a memory of strong arms holding her would intrude. She'd hear his voice whispering erotic suggestions, feel his lips on her naked flesh. The need to be with him again was irresistible.

Just like the night after the movie, when she couldn't drive home no matter how she tried, she now couldn't make the call that would end her affair.

She told herself it was simple courtesy to break up with the man in person. That's what she'd do. She'd go to the hotel and explain why she couldn't see him anymore.

NICK THREW a few things into his overnight bag, but not much, since he left it packed between Fridays. He tossed in his razor and a bottle of scented oil.

His body ached as he imagined rubbing oil into hers, his hands gliding over her curves and hollows, warming her skin, loosening her tight muscles, relaxing her.

Would she even show tonight?

He wasn't certain. He'd thrown a curve ball, asking her out. But as much as he loved these Friday nights, he didn't think he could keep it up. How many times this week at the office had he restrained himself from giving her a kiss, an intimate touch, even a glance, such as lovers share?

He zipped the bag with a jerking hiss. He was going to slip one of these days.

Then she'd hate him.

He took the stairs, pounding down seven floors of cement steps to his apartment's underground parking garage.

Most men would kill for what he had going. A beautiful desirable woman who came to him only for sex. Uncomplicated, no-strings sex.

And, perversely, he was the one who wanted strings. Hell, not strings, thick, unbreakable ropes to bind her to him.

He wanted to take her in the light. He wanted to gaze into her blue eyes as he thrust deep inside her body. He wanted to watch her skin flush as passion overtook her, hear his name on her lips when she cried out in ecstasy.

Tossing his bag into the back of his dark green BMW, he got into the front, shifting slightly to ease the ache of his erection as he bent to get into the car. Sex with Genna was like nothing he'd ever known. But he wanted so much more. He wanted to show her off in public, knowing she was his. All his. Not just one night a week, but every single night.

He was gambling big time, and he knew it. But it was time to move to the next step in his admittedly unconventional plan to win Genna.

As he drove through the busy Friday night traffic he considered the dilemma he'd finessed himself into. He was preparing to have sex with the woman tonight, and a first date with her tomorrow. He snorted in self-disgust. Maybe he should call the hotel and leave her a message, canceling. Put an end to it before she found out. Then, as himself, he could woo her the way he should have done from the beginning.

He reached for his cell, then put it back. Cancel Neptune and have her turn to old buddy Nick on the rebound? Oh, no.

Genna had to choose Nick over Neptune.

Her late-night lover had helped her awaken her own sexuality. Now it was time for her to move on to a real flesh-and-blood man, one who'd make demands on her time and attention. Demands she would want to meet because she cared.

Turning onto North State Parkway, he gripped the steering wheel, hard. Would she make the correct choice?

What was she thinking, his uptight everything-to-schedule Genna? She was pretty straitlaced in her way. He wondered how she'd handle sex on Friday and a date on Saturday. Hell, maybe she'd already canceled on *him*.

Which would definitely mean she was serious about her old pal Nick not being her old pal any longer, but her new lover. A spurt of excitement shot through his gut. Ahead, the light turned red. He stopped, reached once more for his cell and called the hotel.

He received a pang of disappointment for his trouble. There were no messages for Mr. Neptune of room 1604.

She was planning to keep their date. Good news for Mr. Neptune. Not so good for old pal Nick.

He arrived early and strode through the lobby toward the elevator, excitement stirring as he anticipated the hours ahead. A window display in a gift shop caught his eye and he stopped to look. Umbrellas and silk scarves, all printed with various masterpieces from the Chicago Institute of Art, gave him an idea. Well, he could care less about the umbrellas. It was the scarves he perused. He noted one scarf in particular, in shades of blue and purple, that would look great on Genna.

He'd wanted to see Genna while he made love to her. Maybe he'd found a way.

He entered the shop, heading past the miniature bulls, the perfumes, the *I ♥ Chicago* T-shirts to the display window and picked up the silk scarf. It was smooth and cool, a little like the lady it was intended for.

"Ah, you like Renoir," the clerk said as she wrapped the package in tissue and placed it carefully in a gift bag.

"Yes. Very nice." He answered. In truth he hadn't glanced at the actual painting, he'd been thinking of how the blues and purples of the scarf would look against Genna's fair skin and blond hair as he tied it over her eyes.

Once in the room, he took his usual shower and

pulled the hotel robe over his naked body. He un-packed the scented oil, threw a supply of condoms on the bedside table, removed a single magnolia blossom wrapped in damp paper towel and stuck it in a water glass.

The scent of magnolia started giving him ideas, and he gazed at the wrapped scarf, wondering if he'd get a chance to use it.

He tore off the tissue and stuffed the scarf in the pocket of the robe.

He'd brought work to keep him occupied for the half hour or so until she arrived, but he mostly read and then reread what he hadn't taken in, all the while keeping an eye on the clock.

Finally he stopped wasting his time, packed up the work and lay back on the bed with his arms crossed behind his head, his body already erect for her. He was becoming as reliable as Pavlov's dog. All he had to do was think about Fridays at eleven, or get a whiff of magnolia, and his cock grew hard.

It was almost eleven. Even as excitement built in his belly, he hoped she wouldn't come. He wanted Mr. Neptune to be stood up.

For Nick's sake.

He was almost disappointed when the soft knock came.

"Right on time," he muttered to himself as he went to the door and switched off the lights, plunging the room into darkness.

Then she was there, and disappointment had no place. They kissed greedily, starved for each other's touch. Her skin felt cool when he ran his hands over her cheeks, then hot when he yanked the shirt out of her jeans and touched her back. She shivered, and he felt the fine play of muscle beneath the delicate silk of her skin. She was so slender he felt each bump of her spine as his hands traveled up.

Heat seemed to pulse in the air around them; when he breathed, his lungs felt hot. He was so finely tuned to her, he caught the scent of her woman's arousal under the light scent she always wore. Something subtle and floral; he thought of it as eau de corporate woman.

And in the background, like a grace note, the scent of magnolia. The combination made him crazy with lust. Luckily she was wearing some kind of denim shirt with snaps, because he was in no mood for buttons. He needed to get his hands on her flesh.

She sighed, a quiet "Yes," as he bared her upper body.

"I was planning to cancel," she said in a soft voice.

Hope leapt in his chest. Would she give him the kiss-off now? Clearing the way for her to be completely available to Nick? "Why were you going to cancel?" he whispered, rubbing his palms over her breasts, feeling her nipples pebble.

She didn't answer right away. Would she tell him about her date with Nick? With *him* for tomorrow night? Would she now dump her mystery Neptune so she could be with a real man? He hoped quite violently that she would.

At last she spoke, softly as before, but with a hesitancy that was foreign to her. "Do you think of me? During the week?"

Was this leading up to dumping him? He wasn't

an expert, but it didn't sound good so far. Damn it, he wanted her to dump him. The worst of it was he found he couldn't lie to her to make it easier. "Yes," he whispered, pulling her closer and burying his face in her hair as he'd longed to do all week at the office, kissing her with a proprietary right. "I think of you."

Her breath was tremulous against his lips as she kissed him back, her lips soft and full from passion. "I think of you, too."

"What do you think about?"

"How we are together. I don't even know who you are, but I feel like I know you. There's this connection between us, and it scares me."

He felt the tremble in her breath as she sighed the words. He couldn't prevent himself from soothing her. "Don't be afraid."

"I think about this," she said, parting his robe and rubbing her naked breasts seductively against his chest, and he felt himself grow even harder. "But I think about who you are, and I wish I could just call you sometimes. I wonder if you're thinking of me."

Here was the opening he needed. "Maybe you should find yourself a real man," he whispered.

"Maybe I have."

What the hell was that supposed to mean? Was she referring to the Neptune him or the him she knew as Nick? This whole thing was getting way out of hand. If he wasn't already inside Nick's body, he'd punch the guy out for being such a putz.

"Maybe it's time for you to find out who I am. Go ahead, turn on the light." Inside he burned. How would she react when she discovered she was already sleeping with her good pal Nick, the one she'd been nervous about kissing? He held his breath as he waited for her reply, knowing the only thing he might end up kissing was his ass goodbye as she turfed him from her life.

He swallowed, and it sounded noisy in the still room. He felt her move. Was she going for the light? A minute passed. Two. Nothing. It was as dark as before. As dark as the deepest secret.

When she spoke, her voice came from the bed. ''I don't want to know. I don't want this to change. Not yet.''

Couldn't she see that it had already changed?

''Well,'' he said at last, putting the dilemma aside as his physical needs grew more urgent, ''I need to see you.'' He felt his way to the bed, groping in the blackness until he touched her.

''What are you—'' Her breath caught as he teased the silk scarf across her breasts. He was sure he felt the slippery fabric catch on her nipples. Nipples he'd tasted and sucked and nuzzled but never seen. Were they apricot? Dusky red? He needed to know.

''Do you know what this is?''

''It feels like lingerie,'' she said.

''It's a silk scarf. I saw it and thought of you.''

''I'm not really much of a scarf person,'' she said, sounding a little apprehensive. Did she think he was planning to tie her up? He grinned to himself. A fine idea, but not what he had in mind for tonight. She didn't need to know that quite yet, however.

''It's not a fashion accessory.'' He slid the scarf between her breasts, left it there for a moment while he stripped her of her skirt and panties, then continued stroking her with the scarf. Back and forth over her belly then he felt it slow as it slid over her pubic hair.

"What are you going to do with it?" Her voice pulsed with undeniable excitement—and a hint of nerves.

"I'm going to blindfold you."

He smiled at her soft gasp. "You're not going to force-feed me cherry preserves are you?"

He chuckled. "No. I'm going to turn on the light so I can see you. All of you."

She groaned and her body twisted beneath him. Was she turned on or freaked by the idea? Hard to tell. "What if I don't want you to?"

"I'm going to turn on the light anyway. It's up to you. With the blindfold or without."

"Or I could just leave now."

"That would be another option," he agreed.

He could practically hear the wheels whirring away in her head as she processed this new idea. Would she go for it and make herself even more vulnerable to him? Or would she walk away?

The mature man in him knew the best thing would be for her to walk away and start from scratch with "Nick" tomorrow night.

But the mature man wasn't in bed right now, tormented by the need to see the woman he made love to, naked but for a blindfold.

While she worked out all the arguments, pro and con, in her overanalytical head, he cruised her throat with his lips, all the while trailing the silk scarf over her body.

"I don't know," she whispered, sounding extremely turned on.

"If it helps your decision at all, it's a very tasteful scarf. With a print from a Renoir."

"I love the Impressionists," she said, a thread of laughter in her voice. And he knew this was bad news for Nick. Terrific news for Neptune.

"Close your eyes."

"Promise you won't..."

"No cherries. Can't stand 'em. Trust me."

"Yes," she breathed, and even though it was dark, he knew she'd closed her eyes.

He folded the scarf into an oblong shape and tied it round her head, feeling carefully to make sure it covered her eyes. "It's not tight. You can reach up and untie it any time you like."

"Thank you."

"Are you ready?"

She clutched his arm, her small capable hands warm against his flesh. "I hope you won't..."

Act like a wild beast in mating season as soon as he saw her in all her naked glory? "What?"

"Be disappointed."

How could such an idea cross her mind? He kissed her lips beneath the blindfold. "I already know you're beautiful." He kissed her gently once more, feeling the soft breath of a sigh against his lips. "I've felt and kissed and loved every inch of you. Now I need to see you."

She must have heard the sincerity, even in his whisper, for she let go of his arm and slowly he reached for the light switch. It made a loud snap in the room, echoed by her startled gasp.

He blinked at the sudden brightness and for a moment he was almost blinded by the sight of her pale flesh bathed in lamplight. He blinked again and her body was haloed, then his eyes grew accustomed.

"Say something," she said, and he heard the nervousness behind the words. He saw the stiffness in her muscles as she lay still beneath his gaze. Say something. What could he say? He'd guessed she was beautiful under her clothes, the way a man automatically checks out a woman's shape. But he hadn't come close.

"You're more beautiful than I imagined," he whispered, groaning inside at the way he sounded like a drugstore greeting card.

It was the truth though. He'd seen her face countless times and in many moods, but never like this, when her blond hair was tousled, her cheeks delicately flushed with sexual excitement, her lips plump and wet. Her throat was long and graceful. Her shoulders were creamy, her arms lightly muscled.

Her breasts—they were understated. Not particularly large, but round and pert, the nipples dusky, like rose petals in late summer. Oh, man, there he went again spouting nonsense. At least he hadn't said *that* aloud.

"What do you see?" Her wispy tone went straight to his groin. She must feel the worship of his gaze and be basking in it.

Oh, boy. He was going to sound like the whole damn Valentine's Day greeting-card counter. He shrugged. If she was brave enough to lay naked before him with a blindfold over her face, he could be brave enough to make a fool of himself with words.

It was easy to remember to whisper. Her body made him feel reverent. "I see skin the color of cream." He ran just a finger along her collarbone and smiled as her flesh became covered in goose bumps where he touched her. "No, not cream," he corrected himself, coming up at last with the perfect image. "Like magnolia."

She laughed softly, a little more pink deepening her cheeks.

"Pale cream tinged with pink. And right in the middle of the blossom, the pink gets so dark it's almost purple." He touched the crest of her nipples. "That's what color you are here."

Her nipples strained forward and he knelt over her to take first one in his mouth, then the other. She moaned softly as he lapped at each peak then pulled it into his mouth.

He raised his head to watch her body's reaction to his caress, so he could describe it to her. "And where I've sucked them, they darken even more and glisten. Like…like…" Like what? Rubies? Damn, he wished he'd taken poetry as a college elective instead of political science.

As he gazed at her, once again the perfect image popped into his mind. "Like the magnolia after it rains, and the water beads deep inside the blossom making it an even deeper purple."

"Oh," she said, her breathing quickening, making those glorious wet nipples rise and fall so he longed to kiss them again.

So he did. Long and thoroughly, rolling them between his tongue and the roof of his mouth. He heard her soft sighs of pleasure, but even better, he could raise his head and watch her lips part as she sighed, watch her white teeth catch her bottom lip.

His gaze traveled down her body. "I love your stomach."

She giggled, softly, breathlessly. "You do?"

"It's slender, but firm. Like a dancer's."

"I used to take Irish dancing as a kid," she said.

He almost answered, "I know," but stopped himself just in time. "Your belly button is deeper than I thought it would be." He grinned softly. "I could get a whole spoonful of cherry preserves in there."

Her belly rippled as she laughed.

His gaze dropped lower and he swallowed his grin. "And this," he grasped the hair in his hand, giving it a gentle tug that make Genna emit a quivery moan, "I can't even begin to describe how gorgeous you are here."

"Try."

And knowing how much this excited her, he did try. "It's darker than the hair on your head, curlier, and it teases the hell out of me. It's like when a woman wears a negligee you can sort of see through, but not quite. When you lie like this with your legs almost closed, I get a glimpse of something. It's the same color as your nipples. The same color as deep inside a magnolia blossom." And he was never going to be able to look at a magnolia tree again without getting a hard-on.

"But when you open your legs a bit..." He took her thighs gently in his hands and parted them. She didn't resist or help, just lay there and let him open her, "I see all of you. The skin is pinker on the outside, and darker purple as it gets closer to the center."

He settled between her legs and leaned in. He opened her gently with his thumbs and her hips arched off the bed. He had to swallow before he could go on, as her deepest beauty was revealed to him. "And inside, right inside your body, it's an even deeper color. And it glistens."

She whimpered.

"It's like a ruby. Red and sparkling." And very, very precious.

He traced just the rim of her opening with his tongue and she bucked beneath him. "And when I touch you with my tongue, everything gets plumper, and darker." Again he tongued just the edge of her and felt it quiver, like a mouth about to cry.

He moved his thumbs up a little way and spread her there. "I may be taking this magnolia image too far, but I swear, when I spread you just like—"

"Oh, please," she cried, and all thoughts of flowers fled. What was going on here was strictly animal. Her cry of appeal went straight through him, and he put his lips right on that needy little bud and sucked her. He broke the suction and used his tongue to stroke her there. He toured the general area, tasting, nibbling, keeping his eyes greedily open to savor the sight of her spread before him, wet and shivering with mounting desire.

He slipped a finger inside her, then two, stroking her inside with his fingers as he stroked her outside with his tongue. She was a hot, wet vise closing in on him as her passion mounted.

Her hips tossed and thrust against him on the bed and he glanced up to see her head thrashing against the pillow, her breasts arching high. She was becoming slicker and hotter by the second. Tighter and harder she clamped his fingers and then she gave a high, shuddering cry as her body spasmed under his tongue, around his fingers.

His own need was so fierce he grabbed a condom, shoving the thing on with hands that shook, and plunged into her while the last tremors still rocked her.

Then he took her up again, holding her cheeks beneath his palms as he loved her. He couldn't watch her eyes, so he concentrated on her mouth, plump and sexy and wet from his kisses. She mouthed words, but no sound came out of her.

He raised up on his elbows and gazed at her breasts. Her chest was deeply flushed and, he thought, he never would have known orgasm did that to her so long as their loving had remained in the dark.

He watched her head toss about on the pillow, the blindfold a blur of blues and greens as her control slipped. He wanted it to last forever, this ride to heaven, but, in spite of his grandiose impersonation of a sea god, he was only mortal. Adding sight to his other senses was too much. Her fevered excitement was too much.

Thrusting harder, he pushed her up and up until her wordless mouthing became the helpless cries he loved to hear. As much as he wanted to kiss her, he held himself back for the exquisite pleasure of watching her come.

But, at the crucial moment, she dragged his head down and plastered her mouth against his. It was the last straw. Greedily, he kissed her as they both plunged over the edge.

Is it possible to fall in love with someone you've never seen? Genna asked herself as she wandered around her apartment Saturday morning, stunned. Could all these feelings be just from sex?

And how could she date one man, when she could still taste another man on her lips? Feel him against her skin? She had allowed herself to be completely vulnerable to her sea-god lover last night. She'd done something she never recalled doing before—she'd given up control completely.

And she'd really, really liked it.

Now, only a few hours later, she was supposed to get ready for a date with Nick. Why, just when she needed a friend to talk to, why did he have to start showing interest in her as a woman?

She'd planned to break if off with Neptune last night. Instead she'd fallen in love with him.

She vacuumed her condo within an inch of its life, wishing the roar of the machine would drown out her clamoring thoughts. But no matter how hard she scrubbed, dusted, polished or swept, those thoughts wouldn't be silenced.

The phone sat there like a nagging mother. Every time she glanced at it, it seemed to be telling her to call Nick and tell him she couldn't go out with him. No girl with manners dates two men at once.

She slumped on her couch and put her feet up, throwing the cushions she'd meticulously arranged into disarray. If she couldn't break things off with Neptune, she'd have to break things off with Nick before there was anything *to* break off.

She reached for the phone and punched in his number. Except she had trouble seeing the keypad as her eyes filmed with tears.

The phone rang and she willed herself not to hang up.

"Harvard Home Heating," a cheery voice proclaimed.

"I'm sorry," Genna replied on a sob. "I've got the wrong number."

With trembling hands she replaced the phone in its cradle. She'd dialed the wrong number. That must be some kind of a sign she wasn't meant to cancel.

She thought about how much she liked being with Nick. He was smart, sexy and fun, but there was something deeper, something softer that had gradually developed between them. Something she'd only recently noticed.

She couldn't cancel on him.

Oh, hell. She didn't know what she was going to do.

Then she stepped into the shower, her second of the day. As she soaped her body, she heard the echo of a whisper, comparing her breasts and other more intimate parts of her to a Southern magnolia.

Even as she warmed at the memory, she scrubbed harder, as though she could scrub away the things she'd done with a stranger. She didn't want to fall in love with him. She couldn't.

If she wasn't careful she could end up with Tiffany Ross's dilemma, abandoning a flesh-and-blood man to chase after an unattainable fantasy.

Why did she ever go to New Orleans? Why?

If she ever made partner she was going to lobby against all corporate retreats. If the members of the firm had to meet, they could do it in a damn boardroom.

10

GENNA'S BUZZER SOUNDED. Even though she'd been waiting for it, the sound made her drop her purse.

For a crazy moment she thought about not answering it. She could hole up here in her apartment. As long as she did, she didn't have to admit that her relationship with Nick might be changing.

She didn't want it to change.

Did she?

She tried to swallow the nerves crowding her throat. She was nervous—of Nick. Her once orderly life was like a children's carnival ride that had jumped its tracks and taken on a life of its own. And she wanted it back on the tracks!

She pushed the intercom and Nick's voice floated up to her sounding cheerful and strong, just the way it always did. Why wasn't he a bag of nerves?

Suddenly she didn't want him in her apartment, this man who had her key just as she had his, and who'd been in her home countless times. It might send the wrong signal for a first date.

She sighed. Already their friendship had changed.

"I'll come down," she said.

She took the stairs at a walk, prolonging the inevitable by a good forty-five seconds or so. Then there was nothing else to do but greet him at the door.

"Hi," he said. "You look great." They were the words anybody might say, but just as she thought maybe she'd made a huge thing about nothing and started to relax, she glanced up and caught his gaze on her.

There was no misunderstanding the heat in his eyes.

Her heart hammered and a strange feeling washed over her, like a wave of dizziness. She wanted to glance away, but couldn't.

His eyes were silver in the outside light from her building. His thick, wavy hair was freshly brushed and he wore a light summer suit. He looked like an ad for a clothing designer—not one of those androgynous male models with big lips and no facial hair—but a real man.

And he was that, she sighed. A real man. Not a fantasy that could exist in a dark hotel room one night a week. A career stumbling block of gigantic proportions.

She realized he'd made a special effort with his appearance, and again that little niggle of nerves hit her. "Why are we doing this?" she blurted before she could stop herself.

He rolled his eyes. "Because it's healthy to eat three meals a day."

"I'm not talking about eating dinner. I'm talking about—" she gestured helplessly "—this! Us!"

He grabbed her arm as an elderly couple came out of the apartment's front entrance. "Come on," he urged, his eyes losing some of their heat. "Let's walk a bit."

How could he sound so calm and assured when she

felt as if the world had started spinning in the wrong direction?

They walked at a comfortably brisk pace and she heard their shoes slapping the sidewalk, the quiet *whoosh* as a car went by. She felt the soft warm impact every time his shoulder brushed hers.

"What happened to Ms. PR?" she asked, when the silence felt too heavy.

"Who?" She'd swear he'd been miles away and had forgotten she was by his side.

"The PR woman who had her eyes glued to you at Marcy and Darren's party."

"Nothing happened. She wasn't my type."

A little spurt of relief shot through her, which annoyed her so much it made her snarky. "She was sane, you mean."

He let out a long, frustrated sigh. "Okay, cards on the table. Here's the deal. I'm tired of dating those women."

"The boobs, the bods and the bunnies?"

"Some of those women were very nice."

She giggled. This was more like it. Teasing Nick about his awful women, him teasing her about the lack of men in her life. This is how it was best between them, and most comfortable. Her shoulders relaxed as she called up one of her favorite Nick moments. "They sure were. Especially Sugar. Remember her? You brought her to the firm Christmas party and the minute she heard 'Santa Claus is Coming to Town' she started stripping her—"

"Yes. I remember. But you know what I liked about her?"

"I could hazard a couple of guesses."

"She didn't analyze everything to death. She was out to have a good time, and she usually managed. What's wrong with that?"

"It's not exactly deep or satisfying long-term, is it?"

"No, but it was damned satisfying for the short-term." He glanced at his watch as a cab came round the corner, then hailed it.

Satisfying for the short-term. She pondered that as the cab shot through the streets. Like her regular Friday night sex-fest with Mr. Neptune. Ooh, that was more than satisfying, but realistically, what could it be but a short-term thing? She didn't know who he was. Didn't *want* to know. What did that say about Genna?

And if Nick was breaking out of his hit-and-run dating pattern, what did that say about him?

The restaurant was quiet and upscale. Just the kind of place she liked. When they were seated at their table, she noted her silverware was askew and took a moment to straighten it to her satisfaction.

"Dry sherry?" Nick asked her when the drink waiter arrived.

She wanted to say no, and have something completely different. But she did want a dry sherry. She nodded.

So Nick knew her pre-dinner drink preference. She knew his, too. Single malt scotch on the rocks. So what? It didn't mean they were heading for a golden wedding anniversary.

When their drinks came, they managed to pass some time discussing menu items, but once they'd ordered, an awkward pause fell.

She could toss out light dinner conversation, but she didn't want to. They were here now on an official date and she didn't like it. Not one bit. She didn't see why she should make it easy for him. "Why are you doing this?" she almost wailed.

"Doing what?" He knew damn well, but he was taunting her, making her voice her objections.

"You know what. Changing things."

He gazed at her almost as if he felt sorry for her. The compassion in those smoky gray eyes threw her. "Everything changes, Genna. It's part of life. People change, they grow."

"But I liked us just the way we were. As friends."

He set his scotch on the linen tablecloth and leaned forward. "Then consider this fair warning. My feelings for you are more than friendly."

She glanced up, startled by the blunt admission. He was serious. No smirk marred the strong planes of his cheeks, or crinkled the firm fullness of his lips. Their gazes met and held, and she felt again that strange electric buzz. The worst part was she felt as though maybe her own feelings weren't what they'd always been, either.

But she was in love with Neptune. Wasn't she? "But—"

"I know you're scared—"

"Of course I'm not scared."

"You've just rearranged the whole table," he said with the glimmer of a smile. "You sure you're not scared?"

She licked her lips nervously. "I like order."

"You like control."

"I—"

"That's what's scaring you. A real relationship with a man scares you. Because you might lose control."

For a second she was transported back to the night before, when her mystery lover had taken control of her body. She remembered how she'd hated to surrender to the powerful feelings, and how in the end the pleasure had swamped her. She felt her cheeks warm, and hoped the dim lighting would camouflage her blush.

"I just don't approve of office romances."

"Bullshit."

She gasped, feeling annoyance beat the embarrassment coloring her cheeks. "How dare you—"

"People in the firm see us together all the time. Most of them think we're already sleeping together."

"Is that what this is about? Sex?" Even as she said it, in a high-handed, indignant way she'd perfected in high school, heat shot through her belly.

She'd been aware since they sat down of women in the restaurant watching Nick, wishing they were going home with him. He was attractive and sexy, so why did the idea of sleeping with him fill her with panic?

"Partly," he admitted, disconcerting her still further. "I could give you the usual guy's line about wanting to get to know you as a person, but I already know you as a person. And I like you. You can be completely anal and you're a total control freak, but you're also gorgeous, hard-working and decent. I think maybe we could be good together." He shrugged. "And maybe we wouldn't be. But isn't it worth a shot?"

Their meal came then, and Genna could have kissed the waiter for his timing. She had no answer that made sense, either to Nick or to herself. He was right, they had a lot in common and already liked each other. But...

"How's the bouillabaisse?" he asked a few minutes later.

"Delicious," she replied, though for all she tasted anything, she could be slurping mud. "How's the lamb?"

"Terrific."

She sipped wine, only now realizing Nick hadn't ordered any.

"I want to make partner before I'm thirty," she reminded him. "I just don't feel I have enough energy to devote to a relationship right now."

"After you make partner, then what will you use for an excuse?"

"I won't..."

"You will. Partner, judge, president of the United States, there will always be some other goal that gets in your way."

"No. You're wrong. I plan to get married some day."

"Sure, to some poor schmuk who doesn't threaten you. You, my darling, are terrified of intimacy."

She wished he hadn't called her my darling, in that casual way of long-term lovers. It threw her off her stride. Again she thought of the night before. Little did Nick know. She could bloody well write a book about intimacy. Fantastic, legendary, orgasm-to-your-toes intimacy. "I *can* be intimate. I have been intimate."

"I'm not talking physical intimacy. I'm talking about two people who mesh, who are intellectually and emotionally connected. Two people who complete each other, who are stronger together than they are apart. Are you sure you've experienced that kind of intimacy? That kind of love?"

He spoke so passionately, she was startled. How did he know so much about intimacy anyway? Was he talking about when he'd almost married Marcy?

"You're terrified that you might fall in love with me. Then you'd be giving up some of your precious control."

Fall in love with him? As if. She took a big gulp of wine ready to really let him have it, swallowed, then glanced up. But that was Nick sitting across from her, Nick who liked nothing more than to incite her into crazy arguments. Her outrage turned to amusement.

She laughed. "You know, this is the strangest first date I've ever been on. I mean, I've been bored half to death, hit on, spilled on and grossed out, but I've never been threatened with love before."

Answering humor glittered in his eyes, and she remembered why they were such good friends. They "got" each other.

NICK WATCHED Genna laugh at the idea of loving him, and he let it go. He'd given her enough to think about for one night. He knew her; she'd mull over everything they'd said, analyze it to death, probably write a damn brief about it.

He'd taken the first step. The next was up to her.

And, he thought, I may lose her in the end, but at least I'm giving it my best shot.

She'd escaped behind her corporate-woman-on-a-first-date mask, and he didn't try to roust her out, but let her return to her emotional comfort zone. Even as she led them into safe subjects, he thought, *There is no safe subject when I'm with you. Every word sounds like a caress and puts me in greater danger of falling under your spell.*

He watched her suck the meat out of a prawn and his mouth went dry with memories she didn't know they shared. Watched her hands grasp the stem of her wineglass and remembered... Oh, hell. They should be going home together after dinner. They were so right and natural together. Damn the woman for being so stubborn and so completely out of touch with her own needs.

There was sudden silence and he realized she'd stopped talking. He heard the clink of cutlery, laughter and the buzz of conversation all around them, but there was an odd quiet at their table.

"I thought you liked the lamb?"

Is that what was on his plate? He'd forgotten. "I do," he answered her.

"You stopped eating. You were just staring at me with this funny look on your face."

"I was thinking how beautiful you look on a date. It's a new one on me."

"Thank you." She took her bottom lip between her teeth and he wished he'd bitten his own tongue off before he blurted something that would toss her right back out of her comfort zone.

She put down her spoon and reached for her wine.

She sipped and swallowed, and even though his stomach was knotted waiting for her to speak, he couldn't help but notice the wine glistening on her lips when she took the glass away, could barely resist the urge to lean across the table and kiss the wetness off her lips.

"Nick, I'm...I'm..." She took a deep breath and he opened his mouth to tell her to just shut the hell up. He didn't want her to finish that sentence. But even as he tried to form words, she straightened and spoke in a clear voice. "I'm seeing someone else."

Once, back in high school, when he'd played soccer for the Italian-American Junior League, an opposing player's boot connected with his gonads. He felt something similar now. It was a curious mixture of intense pain and getting the wind knocked out of your lungs, so you couldn't even yell out your hurt.

"Who is he?" As if he didn't know.

Her blush reminded him of his nonsense about comparing her to a magnolia blossom. Would she tell him about her Friday night special?

If she did, would he do some confessing of his own?

But it seemed their friendship had changed. Where once she would have told him, now she dropped her gaze and lined up the bread rolls in the basket.

"It's no one you know," she muttered.

Like hell, he wanted to roar. "Is it serious?"

She glanced up and he saw the confusion in her eyes. "I don't know. I...maybe."

He was so jealous he wanted to commit violence. Except the man he was jealous of was himself.

There ought to be some kind of spectacular booby

prize for what he'd just done. He'd stolen his own woman.

GENNA WAS LATE FOR WORK.

For most people this would not be newsworthy, but for Genna it was as good as broadcasting to the world that she was slipping. She'd overslept, arisen heavy-eyed and groggy, taken an all-time worst getting-ready time of twenty-seven minutes, run her panty hose and had no time to go back and change.

Now she stumbled into work feeling tired and off-kilter. Both feelings could be traced to the same source.

Nick Cavallo.

A burning sense of injustice bubbled through her system as she contemplated how happy she'd been with their friendship. Now, just when she was trying to sort out her complicated secret love life, Nick further complicated it. He didn't want to be friends anymore, he wanted to be romantically involved.

She was so confused she was having trouble concentrating, torn by conflicting feelings and images. Nick laughing at her while he fixed her kitchen faucet. Nick giving her a post-date good-night kiss days *before* their date.

When she thought of these things she wondered if she was a fool to turn him down.

Then she'd imagine her mystery lover worshipping her body with his lips, making her feel things she didn't know she was capable of feeling. And she realized he was important to her, too.

Of course, Nick had taken her brush-off—if that's what you could call it—well.

For a second there, after she'd told him there was someone else in her life, he'd looked almost violent. Then he'd shrugged and offered her a crooked grin that made her heart lurch. "Remember, whatever happens, I'm still your friend."

That was what she wanted, of course, to have him as her friend again, but somehow she didn't believe him. They'd crossed a line and, like the undefended border of a friendly country, she hadn't even noticed when they'd crossed. All she knew was she didn't think they could ever go back.

She all but staggered to her office, feeling the beginning of a dull headache. Coffee, she needed coffee. Intravenous espresso drip would be best, but the coffee-room brew was her only option.

She schlepped to the coffee room and froze halfway.

Nick was standing with his back to her, chatting with somebody. He had an arm curled atop a file cabinet, and her gaze was drawn to the way that upraised arm pulled the muscles of his back taut under the crisp white dress shirt.

His legs were long and muscular, his butt round and firm from all the years he'd played soccer. His thick dark hair was just starting to curl over the back of his collar. In the old days, even a week ago, she'd have joined the conversation, nagged him to get his hair cut.

But now she just stood there, gawking at him, while an unfamiliar sensation washed through her.

Longing.

But even as she acknowledged that longing, she felt disloyal to Neptune. She had feelings for her secret lover, and she believed he had feelings for her, too. It wasn't something they ever talked about, but when their bodies communicated on that most intimate level, there was something sweet and sharp and strong that made her eyes sting.

She stood there with her empty coffee mug and felt more miserable and confused than she'd ever felt in her life.

Unable to face him yet, she decided to sneak back into her office before Nick spotted her.

"Morning, Genna, rough night?" Her secretary, Maureen, greeted her loudly.

She jumped and mumbled something.

Even as she hoped against hope that Nick hadn't heard and she could sneak back to her office, he turned and his gaze ran over her in surprise. She felt like throwing the damn mug at him. He, of course, looked relaxed and unflapped by their aborted date.

"You ripped your nylons," he said as she stomped past to the coffee room.

"You need a haircut," she snapped back.

Of course, the pot was empty when she got there. And, of course, she couldn't leave and slink back to her own office without going past Nick, so she slapped together a fresh pot, feeling her mood grow blacker than the old coffee grounds she tossed.

She heard footsteps behind her on the tile floor and didn't have to turn around. She knew it was Nick. Stubbornly, she remained facing the coffeemaker, just wishing he'd go away.

"You got my memo?"

"Yes. The judge wants a status conference in Ross versus Ross. Friday at three o'clock in judge's chambers.'' She virtually repeated his memo word for word.

"Is everything all right?'' He sounded so sympathetic and caring. As if it wasn't all his fault.

"Friends ask questions like that. You're not my friend anymore, remember?'' The minute the words left her mouth she wished she could call them back. She sounded petulant and immature.

"Genna...'' There was concern in his tone, even a kind of pain. In spite of herself she turned to him.

His eyes were serious, unsmiling as they gazed at her. His chest was broad, his shoulder just the right height for leaning on, but, she reminded herself, he was the reason she felt like this. He wasn't a shoulder to lean on anymore. "Don't listen to me,'' she groaned. "I'm just tired and bitchy. I didn't—'' She stopped herself before she could admit she hadn't slept properly since she last saw him. "I didn't get to bed until late last night.'' That was better. Maybe he'd think she'd been with the other man she'd hinted at.

The coffee machine gurgled and sputtered behind her and the glorious smell of freshly brewed coffee filled the room, and still he gazed at her. He propped a hip against the counter, leaning his bronzed hands against it. "Maybe I was wrong,'' he said at last. "Maybe we can just go back to the way things were before.''

She filled her mug slowly, then turned without conscious thought and topped his mug. "Maybe it's too late to go back,'' she said slowly, feeling an unaccustomed stinging behind her eyelids, and left the room.

11

GENNA'S STOMACH was as wobbly as though *she* were the one getting divorced.

As she sat beside Nick, feeling as if her fantasy lover had destroyed her prospects with a real man, Genna understood how Tiffany, sitting on her other side, must feel.

Maybe the young mother was no rocket scientist, but she loved her husband and loved her kids. She'd been foolish, not criminal, and she didn't deserve to lose so much.

In the back of her head a little voice whispered, it was nothing but a fantasy that got out of hand. Fantasies, Genna was forcefully reminded, could be damaging. And the real-life fantasy she herself was indulging in every Friday night was a perfect example. She was rejecting a flesh-and-blood man she liked because she couldn't step away from her obsessive attraction to a stranger.

And to think she used to pride herself on being sensible. She unpacked her briefcase, slapping papers onto the table.

Across the table sat Rory Ross and his lawyer, a copy of the P.I.'s report aggressively displayed with the front cover facing the empty seat at the head of the conference table, where the judge would sit.

Genna felt Nick beside her, felt his warmth, heard the shuffle of papers as he arranged documents in front of him just as she had. But she refused to glance his way. She didn't want to gaze at his profile. Certainly didn't want to catch his eye.

Instead, she focused on Tiffany Ross. Their client had obviously made an effort with her appearance today. Her hair curled softly about her face, styled in a new cut that made her appear younger. She wore a muted floral summer dress with pearls in her ears and at her throat. Her makeup was soft and tasteful. The only splash of color was the defiantly bright red of her lipstick.

Playing with her pearls with pink-nailed fingers, Tiffany gazed at her husband.

"Don't worry, it's going to work out," Genna said, reaching under the table to clasp her other hand. She wondered which one of them she was trying to reassure.

Tiffany's hand was clenched and icy cold. "Thanks," she murmured, giving Genna a wobbly smile. Genna was glad she'd remembered to stuff a brand-new box of tissue in her briefcase.

Mr. Ross's lawyer, a fresh-faced young man she'd seen a few times but never met, tapped his fingers rhythmically against the table.

Mr. Ross himself studied his fingernails, which gave Genna opportunity to study him. A thickset man in his late thirties, he shifted his broad shoulders in a cheap suit that didn't fit him at all. She wondered if he'd borrowed it.

His hair was cut very short, his features good, although his mouth was drawn down in anger. She guessed there was at least one tattoo under the ill-fitting suit and that he'd be fat within a decade.

She wondered what their client—she of the wealthy family and trust fund—saw in him, and would have shaken her head at the strange impulses of the mating ritual. Except Rory chose that moment to lift his head.

And he stared straight at Tiffany. The expression of pain and passion in his gaze scorched the air between them.

Quickly, Genna gave Nick a subtle jab with her elbow and motioned with her chin in Mr. Ross's direction.

Nick turned to look and she saw his eyes widen at the display.

Rory Ross was like a young Brando. Any moment she expected him to bellow "Tiffa-nee" in a wounded-bull roar.

She heard Tiffany's soft gasp from her other side, but her own attention was now on Nick. She watched him in profile as he stared at Mr. Ross. One gray eye narrowed, as she knew his gaze did when he concentrated. A few deep laugh lines fanned out from the corners. His forehead was high, with a black lock of hair falling across it that she itched to smooth back.

His nose was unquestionably Italian. Longish with a definite roundness at the end. His lips were firm, his chin more so. Stubborn in fact. Tiny black dots in his olive skin indicated his five-o'clock shadow was making an early appearance.

Then he turned to her and suddenly the gray eyes were gazing at her. Clear, intelligent gray eyes with thick black lashes most women would kill for.

"Interesting," he said, jerking his chin in Rory Ross's direction.

She nodded. "He still loves her," she said softly, as Judge Timmins entered the room.

Judge John Timmins was not one to waste time. A devoted family man and the father of six kids, he was always irritable during divorce cases. Since Genna's side didn't want the divorce, she couldn't be happier he was hearing their case.

"Good afternoon," the judge said, slipping reading glasses on. His grizzled black curls showed plenty of gray, and his face was set in tired lines. He placed two briefs in front of him.

"Mr. Ross says his wife committed adultery and wants a quick divorce. Mrs. Ross says she didn't commit adultery and doesn't want a divorce at all. Does that sum up the situation?"

He glanced at them over his glasses with sharp brown eyes.

"Yes, sir," said Nick.

"Your Honor," said the young lawyer on the other side, "my client is shattered by his wife's infidelity. He wants matters resolved quickly so that he and his children can get on with their lives."

Beside her, Tiffany gave a choked cry. *Welcome to the world of divorce law, kid.*

Rory Ross glanced at his wife, then a dull red painted his cheeks as he went back to contemplating the table in front of him.

"I am not convinced that Mrs. Ross did in fact commit adultery," said the judge.

"We have a private investigator's report sir, which clearly states—"

"It clearly states that Mrs. Ross entered the apartment building inhabited by several people including a man she had lunch with. I saw no evidence of intercourse."

Mr. Ross squirmed and his big hands gripped the edge of the table as though to hold himself in place.

Sniffling sounds erupted on Genna's left. She reached in her briefcase and handed Tiffany the box of tissues.

"But the evidence—"

"Is circumstantial, and Mrs. Ross has a signed affidavit from Mr. Chance, the man she was seen with. He confirms the two were never intimate."

Mr. Ross's lawyer snorted. "Mr. Chance also agreed to sign an affidavit for us confirming he *did* consummate his relationship. He wanted five thousand dollars. *We* declined his services."

Knowing Nick, Genna grabbed for his arm but was too late. He was already on his feet. "What are you suggesting?"

"I'm suggesting—"

"Gentlemen, please," the judge interrupted testily. "You can take this to the back alley when we're done. Mr. Cavallo, sit down."

Nick glared a moment longer at his opponent and then sat, but Genna felt his frustration. Simon Chance's signed declaration had just lost all credence.

The judge gathered the papers together and tapped them against the table. Tiffany sniffled nonstop beside Genna. Mr. Ross loosened his tie as though it were choking him and his lawyer looked like a kid who'd just won at marbles.

"Judge Timmins," Nick said into the charged silence, "may I ask Mr. Ross a few questions?"

Every gaze turned on Nick. His eyes were the flat gray of a gun barrel, and she felt sorry for the cocky young lawyer if he ever did face Nick in an alley. She wondered what Nick was up to. He hadn't discussed this with Genna. Perhaps he was acting on instinct, based on Rory Ross's unguarded expression earlier.

"All right," said the judge.

"Mr. Ross. Were you happy in your marriage?"

"Yeah. It wasn't me who—"

"Did you ever fantasize about other women?"

"Your Honor, this is outrageous. My client's not on trial."

"No one's on trial. There's no jury, no decisions will be made today. I'll decide what's outrageous in my chambers. You keep your mouth shut. Answer the question, Mr. Ross."

He flushed an even deeper shade. "No."

Nick flipped through some papers and selected one. "It's normal for a sexually healthy male." He emphasized the words *sexually healthy*. "Are you sure you don't fantasize, Mr. Ross?"

The man shot a glance at his wife then away again. "Well, maybe once in a while."

"It's common for a man, while making love to his wife, to fantasize that she's—" Nick paused and shrugged, his voice lilting a question "—Madonna?"

"Not me. I like that one that was married to Tom Cruise."

"So you fantasize about Nicole Kidman when you make love to your wife."

"Yeah. That's the one. And there's an exercise gal on TV, can't remember the name..."

"Rory!" Tiffany stopped sniffling and glared at her husband.

"Well, just maybe once or twice. Mostly I think about you, babe," he said, looking harassed and hot. He pulled at the knot on his tie.

"Do you love your wife, Mr. Ross?"

Rory's lawyer leaned toward him, but was too late.

"Hell, yeah. I just wish she hadn't have done that."

"Could you forgive your wife for having a fantasy?"

Mr. Ross sputtered, but couldn't seem to form a coherent word.

Nick turned to Tiffany. "Do you love your husband, Mrs. Ross?"

"Ye-es," she hiccupped. "I never would have slept with him, Rory. I wouldn't. We just talked. I pretended I was interesting." She sniffed. "It was stupid."

"I've heard enough," said the judge. "I'm suggesting one month of marriage counseling."

"But, Your Honor," Mr. Ross's lawyer protested.

"I don't want you living together. At the end of a month, if you still want the divorce, you can sit down with your lawyers and hammer out an agreement, or I'll see you in court for the divorce hearing.

"Is that acceptable to you, Mr. Ross?"

"I guess so."

"Mrs. Ross?"

"Yes, sir."

Judge Timmins rose and glanced from one to the other. "I hope you work things out. Good day."

"MADONNA, HUH?" Genna said to Nick over the rim of her margarita glass. She was so happy that Tiffany Ross had a chance to save her marriage that she'd wanted to kiss Judge Timmins.

She also wanted to kiss Nick, but knew that was a bad, bad idea, so she teased him instead.

Nick looked smug and relaxed with his shirtsleeves rolled up and the top button of his shirt undone. His suit jacket hung crookedly over the back of his chair, a tongue of red silk tie hanging out the pocket. Even though the bar was noisy, it was still strangely intimate, surrounded as they were by a crowd of Friday night afterwork strangers.

"What can I say? Rory looked like the Madonna type."

She leaned closer. "Are you sure *you're* not the Madonna type?"

He turned the full force of his gaze on her. "You know what type I am."

Her own suit jacket hung on her chair back, a little more neatly than his, and under her tank top she felt strange pitter-patters, as if her heart was stammering. She tried to shrug and ignore his obvious implication. "When I collected research about sexual fantasy, I never thought you'd use it against Rory Ross."

"I saw him checking out your body when you first sat down. That's what gave me the idea."

"Ee-ew, what a jerk."

Nick shrugged. "Can't blame a guy for looking."

His action suited his words. He was looking at her in a way that made her pull in a ragged breath.

"I'm glad the research came in useful," she said, trying to steer the conversation back to neutral ground.

"Haven't you ever wondered why we work so well together?"

"Because we're both brilliant?" She grinned and sipped her margarita.

"Besides that."

A frown of concentration pulled her brows together as she tried to find a serious answer. "I think it's because we both care. I mean, you really wanted that couple to work it out, didn't you?"

He leaned back, and she noticed the dark shadow of his chest hair underneath the white dress shirt, giving her the sense of the animal in him putting on the costume of civilization. "Yeah. I really wanted that one to work."

"Why?" Her mouth felt suddenly dry. Must be too much salt on the rim of her glass. She licked her lips and tasted salt crystals and his gaze followed the path of her tongue with predatory hunger.

"Maybe I thought it would be a sign."

There was a pause. He waited until she asked, "What kind of sign?" Her voice was huskier than the tequila she'd been drinking.

"A sign that you and I were meant to be together."

His gaze was intense and so serious she couldn't turn this comment off with a joke. As she gazed back at him, shock sent goose bumps rippling across her skin. Not because of what Nick had said, but because of her reaction to his words.

At that moment it felt as though a blindfold had fallen from her eyes and she was able to see this man clearly for the first time.

She loved him.

How it had snuck up on her, or even when, she couldn't say. But she knew, with a certainty that frightened her, that she loved Nick Cavallo.

She saw clearly now that she'd used her mystery lover as a way to avoid facing her growing feelings. And yet, he was somehow part of this. Her secret Neptune had helped her face up to her own needs.

Maybe a man in her life wouldn't make her weaker. Maybe he would make her stronger. Especially if that man were Nick.

"Do you really think we were meant for each other?" The bar was noisy and crowded and smelled like beer and old wood, but at this little table in the corner it was intimate and private.

For an answer he leaned closer slowly, giving her all the time in the world to avoid his kiss.

Instead of moving away or turning her head, she leaned toward him, feeling the rightness of being with him. The need to feel his lips on hers.

The noise in the bar faded, the lights seemed to dim as her eyes fluttered shut, she felt his warmth as he neared and then the soft brush of his lips, warm as a promise against hers.

"Mmm," she sighed as he angled his body closer. She felt his hand warm and strong against her back as the heat and pressure of his lips increased.

"'Nother margarita?" came the cocktail waitress's strident voice.

With a jerk Genna pulled back, but the woman

didn't seem fazed. She must see couples necking here all the time. "Uh, no, thanks."

The woman raised her eyebrows, silently asking Nick the same question.

He shook his head and the waitress moved to the next table.

All at once, Genna wished she could call the woman back. If they were done with the drinks, what was next? It seemed inevitable that the night would end in intimacy. And Genna was suddenly terrified. The very thing she'd tried so hard to avoid now seemed as right, as inevitable, as it was frightening. What if they were terrible in bed together? What if he was disappointed? What if...

"Want to dance?"

She'd been so busy worrying, she hadn't even heard the music change. And yet, as though the song had come from the deepest part of her brain, wherever the guilt was locked up, she heard the strains of "You Can Keep Your Hat On."

She'd started to nod and had half-risen from her seat. Then she sat down with a bump, feeling as if the breath had been vacuumed out of her lungs. Oh, no. Not the song that immediately took her back to the first night she'd made love to her whispering stranger.

"I always think of this as a stripper's song," she managed weakly. She still recalled the thrill she'd experienced doing a strip tease in the pitch dark hotel room in New Orleans, and the same erotic thrill began to curl inside her belly.

Nick grinned at her wickedly, gesturing toward the

small dance floor. "Don't let me stop you. I'll just sit back and watch."

She glanced at Nick, knowing now that she loved him, wondering when her good friend had wormed his way into her heart. But the thing that was causing the simultaneous hot flashes and cold shakes was the knowledge that she also loved her nameless whispering stranger.

And today was Friday. Her weekly sex date.

With the familiar stripper's music blaring in her ear, the taste of salt and tequila still on her tongue, she gazed at Nick, so darkly handsome in the dim light of the club. It was time to stop playing games. Time to grow up and accept that she was a woman as well as a lawyer on the partner track. She had a woman's desires, a woman's needs.

Maybe Nick and she would never attain the heights she'd scaled with her midnight lover, but Nick was real. A relationship with him would be real. A shiver rippled over her body at the thought.

It would be as real as smelly socks on the bathroom floor, arguments about where to spend their holidays. As real as children and mortgages and a home in the suburbs.

Her breath came quicker. As real as someone to wake up to in the morning. As real as someone to love, to share her life with. No more sneaking in and out of a dark room, as though her sex life were a dirty secret.

"Are you okay?" Nick leaned forward and touched her shoulder. The warm pressure of his hand on the naked flesh where the tank top ended sent an entirely different shiver through her.

"Yes." She forced a smile. "I'm fine. It's just noisy in here."

He nodded. "Let's go."

She rose and slipped into the suit jacket he held for her.

He took her hand as they left and it felt so right. So warm and sure and absolutely right, that she sighed and allowed herself to lean into him.

"Can I take you to dinner?" he asked as they reached the street.

What if she just said yes?

It was the simplest way. If she didn't show up for her Friday night date, Neptune would get the message.

But she couldn't do it. Even though he was a stranger to her in many ways, he was also her lover and she cared about him. He deserved an explanation. He deserved to know that he had helped her accept that her sexuality was as much a part of her as her time management skills.

The El train roared overhead as they walked the few blocks to the office. "I…can't."

She glanced up at him just as they were passing under a streetlight. Maybe it was a trick of the light, but his eyes took on an almost devilish gleam.

"Hot date?"

Normally she was cool and articulate under fire. Tonight she couldn't seem to stop herself flushing like a teenager, and fumbling for the simplest sentences. She was, in short, a basket case. "It's not exactly…well, it is a sort of a date."

"Can't you blow the guy off?"

It was so close to what she'd been thinking that her

mouth fell open. "I could, but it wouldn't be very polite." She turned to him, eager to explain, and as soon as she was facing him and had his full attention, she found herself tongue-tied once more.

How could she possible explain what she'd been up to? It would sound ludicrous. "I'd like to Nick, but I can't. It's hard to explain, but I have no way of getting hold of him. He'll be expecting me, and I'd like to tell him in person that..."

"That?" he prompted. He still held her hand, and if anything, it felt even warmer than before.

As she said the words, she knew she was making a promise to Nick. A promise that she was willing to move from friends to lovers. "That..." She almost choked and had to stop to clear her throat and then try again. "That I can't see him anymore."

His thumb stroked slow circles on her palm so she had even more trouble thinking straight. "I like the sound of that," he said with a slow seductive smile that made her toes quiver as they attempted to curl over on themselves inside her navy pumps.

"How about tomorrow night?" she said.

"How about come here." He pulled her toward him until her body was flush against his, then he lowered his head and took her mouth. Possessively, hungrily, letting her taste the full force of his desire.

It was so...familiar. She'd always secretly believed that someday she'd meet her soul mate and have this devastating sense of recognition. But she'd never imagined his kiss would seem so familiar, as though she'd kissed just this mouth in just this way hundreds of times. But so it seemed.

He almost reminded her of...but that was crazy.

Love was addling her common sense. Nick would never sneak around pretending to be a stranger when she saw him every day. He wouldn't betray their friendship that way.

Then he deepened the kiss and all thoughts of her secret lover flew from her mind. There was just Nick and her on a city street corner on a sultry summer evening. The air was hot and dry and she smelled dust hanging lazily in the still air.

Just as she grew breathless and weak at the knees, he broke the contact, giving them both a moment to draw breath.

He held her face between his warm palms and gazed into her eyes. "I want you. I care about you. Remember that."

He sounded so intense, so serious that a little shiver of something—anticipation? fear?—swept over her.

12

WHAT THE HELL was he going to do? Nick paced his apartment. His Friday-night bag, already packed, was hunched by the front door like an evil omen. He kicked it across the slate foyer, cursing his own stupidity.

An intelligent man would leave a message at the hotel telling Genna he couldn't make it. Ever again.

Simple, elegant, no strings, no mess.

He crossed to the phone and picked it up. The dial tone buzzed in his ear before he slammed the phone back in its cradle.

If he canceled on Genna, forever more he'd feel like he had a dirty secret he was keeping from her. He couldn't do that, not to the woman he loved. Besides, for both their sakes, she needed to choose Nick over Neptune.

Why the hell did I start the masquerade in the first place? It was a question he couldn't answer. It had seemed logical in New Orleans, when she'd as good as told him she was obsessed by him. Only she hadn't known it was him. The temptation had been irresistible. And now, as so often happened, giving into temptation carried a hefty price tag.

He cursed his mother and grandmother for teaching him to respect women. Well, he tried to curse them, but he couldn't do it—he respected the women in his family too damn much.

Cursing himself for a fool was much easier to do.

So he'd show up. Listen to what Genna had to say when she finally, at long last, dumped Neptune in favor of Nick.

He'd ask her one more time if she wanted to see Neptune in the light.

She'd say no, just as she always did.

Then he'd be off the hook. It wouldn't be him keeping a dirty secret from her; it would be Genna's choice that the secret remain just that. He'd respect her decision. And out of respect he'd never tell her it had been him she'd slept with all those nights. That was the manly thing to do.

The gentlemanly thing.

And his mother and grandmother better never find out or he'd be as popular as yesterday's meatballs.

His gut tightened as he tossed his bag into the car and headed out to his Friday-night rendezvous. Early, as usual, he didn't bother to strip and shower as was his custom. He merely dropped his bag on the king-size bed and started to pace.

Never had he been this nervous, not even when he'd pled a death-row case.

Of course, this time it was *his* life on the line.

In between pacing, he watched the hotel clock as it moved in slow motion, crawling as though mortally wounded toward eleven. He was as glued to the bloody thing as New Year's Eve revelers to the clock at Times Square. After an eternity, the LED display on the hotel clock glowed eleven.

His heart sped up and his skin started to prickle.

But no knock sounded on the door.

If anything, he became even more tense as the minutes continued to crawl.

But by ten after eleven he was feeling pretty damn good. She hadn't showed. If she'd wanted to know who was meeting her in room 1604 every Friday night, all she had to do was ask. And to do that she'd have to have shown up.

Which she hadn't.

With a deep breath of thankfulness, he realized how much he hadn't wanted her to be here tonight. Now, starting tomorrow, he was a free man.

Genna was a free woman.

As far as he was concerned, the whole Neptune affair was a deeply buried, and very pleasant, memory.

He whistled as he grabbed his bag off the bed and headed for the door.

His hand was just touching the knob when he heard the knock. Not only heard it, but felt the vibrations right through his hand.

Viciously, and silently, he cursed.

He tossed his bag into a corner, slapped off the lights and retreated behind the door as usual. Slowly he opened it, glad she couldn't see his fierce scowl in the dark.

"Hi," she whispered softly as she entered and let him shut the door behind her.

"Hi," he whispered back.

She stood there as though waiting for something, and dimly he recalled that he always jumped her the second she was inside, kissing the breath out of her with the eagerness he'd barely kept in check since the week before.

Not tonight, though. He'd kissed her earlier as himself and that had been on the upside of glorious. He wasn't about to go back to kissing her—or doing anything else—as a faceless, nameless nobody.

Hell with it.

Of course, they didn't have much of a protocol. If he didn't jump her bones, they didn't have much of a social act to fall back on.

He did his best, though. "Do you want a drink or something?" he whispered. Polite but lame, he had to admit.

"No." There was a pause. "Thanks for asking."

"Have any trouble parking?" What the hell was wrong with him? Small talk? Now?

"No. I had a valet park my car."

"Good idea." He ran a hand through his hair, glad she couldn't read his expression, even as he wished he could see hers. What was going on in that beautiful head? Was she going to blow him off or wasn't she?

Because if she wasn't, he certainly wasn't going to play the fool for anyone.

Least of all himself.

"Is anything wrong?" she asked, sounding uncertain.

Wrong? He felt like bellowing, *You're supposed to be giving me my walking papers, dumping me, reading the Dear John letter. Get to it!*

Maybe she wasn't planning to dump her stranger after all. Maybe she wanted to have her cake and eat it, too. With a heavy heart he headed toward where she still stood, just inside the door. His hands found her unerringly in the dark, cupping her face and holding her still for his kiss.

As his lips closed over hers he heard her familiar sigh, felt the softening of her body as it leaned into his. For several moments there was no sound but the soft wet suction of kisses given and taken, the quiet shush of clothing rubbing against clothing. The internal sound of rising passion beating against the inside of his skull.

He kissed her.

She kissed him.

It was impossible to tell where one mouth ended and the other began. "This has to be the last time," she finally sighed into his mouth. "I want to tell you goodbye, properly."

For a second, in his desire-fogged brain, he felt irate that she would want to walk away from something so spectacularly good as their lovemaking. "What do you mean, goodbye?" His tongue swooped deep into her mouth, possessively.

"I've met someone," she managed, when he retreated from her.

"Someone new?" Damned if he'd make this easy for her.

She was silent, kissing him back, stepping forward and pushing him back toward the bed. "No. Not exactly. Someone I've known for a while. Someone I'm…serious about."

Yes! About damn time, was what he wanted to say. What he actually said was, "Tell me about him."

"No. You might know him."

"Don't mention his name. Tell me what you like about him."

"This is very weird."

"No. Really. I want to know."

She sighed and pulled her mouth away from his, moving to undo the buttons of his shirt. The shirt she'd seen him in most of the day. How odd that she didn't recognize him even in the dark. Or did she on some level?

"He's a good man."

"Do you love him?"

Now what had made him ask a damn fool question like that? He thought she wouldn't answer. Didn't expect her to in a million years.

"Yes." The answer came soft and low and her voice trembled with it as though the very concept frightened her. As he knew it did.

His throat felt tight. *She loved him.* "He's a lucky man."

"I don't know. What would he think if he could see me now?"

"That you're beautiful. Wild and free. A woman of enormous passion."

She laughed softly. "No. I'm not any of those things. Except with you. Then I can be free. Why is that?"

"Because this is who you really are. No pretense, just you, a woman, and me, the man who loves you."

She gasped, and he realized the words had come out of his mouth unbidden.

"Look, that's not exactly what I—"

There was a sound—even in the dark he recognized it—it was the sound above all others that drove a spike of dread into his gut. The sound of a woman's sob.

"I love you, too. That's what's so awful." She sniffed, and he heard the mattress sigh as she sat on the bed.

He sat beside her, closer to the head of the bed, and tried vainly to comfort her by patting her on the back. "We both knew this had to end."

"But I must be out of my mind. How can I be in love with two men? How can I be in love with a man I've never even seen?" Her voice rose and she hic-coughed on a sob. "I really think I am insane."

He'd do anything to comfort her. Anything at all.

And, he realized, his earlier rationalization for not telling her who he was had been bogus and cowardly. Nick and Genna couldn't start out together until he'd been completely open with her.

He had to turn on the light.

Heart pounding he turned her face toward him, feeling the wetness of a tear tickle his thumb.

"Genna," he said gently, very deliberately not whispering. "You're not insane."

Her whole body stiffened beside him. "Your voice—it's so..."

"Familiar?" He leaned forward, knowing this was the moment he'd longed for as much as he'd dreaded it. Now she'd see him and know him. No more sneak-ing around pretending to be a stranger when he damn well wasn't. From now on he and Genna were out in the open, under the spotlight. Bring on the midday sun.

He snapped on the light. Then he turned to her, a tender smile of welcome on his lips and prepared to take her in his arms.

He heard her gasp.

He leaned forward.

She punched him in the face.

"Ow!" he cried, instinctively covering his throbbing eye with one hand. The other eye was blurry with a haze of pain, but he could see even through the blur that Genna wasn't taking this well.

"You scum!" she yelled. "You low, contemptible, cheating, lying bastard!"

"Genna, stop!" he shouted as she stomped toward the door. "I love you."

She yanked the door open and turned to glare at him. "Well, I hate you."

He rose unsteadily, determined to stagger after her.

"Don't you dare try to follow me. I'll never forgive you. Never."

The words hadn't finished echoing before the door shut with quiet fire-door efficiency, closing the door on the love of his life without so much as a slam.

13

WHACK. THE TINY BLACK rubber ball squealed in protest as it smashed against the wall, flying down the side wall like a bullet and dropping, spent, in the unreachable sweet spot in the corner.

Marcy groaned as her racket clattered against the wall in a futile attempt to return Genna's shot. She bent forward and a drop of sweat splashed to the scuffed wooden floor. "Your point," she wheezed.

The ball was hot to the touch as Genna served again with the power of a superhero. For several minutes there was no sound but the grunt of breath expelled, the slap and squeal of the ball against the walls of the squash court.

Anger had given her strength like she'd never known. All she had to do was picture Nick's face on the ball to send it ricocheting off the walls, pulverized time and again by her racquet.

"I need a break!" Marcy panted at the end of the second game. Genna had won both, a first in their friendship.

As they chugged water and dragged in air outside the court, her best friend stared at her. "What demon got into you?" She mopped her flushed face and neck with a towel.

Genna opened her mouth to speak and a red tide

of fury blinded her. "I can't talk about it yet. I'm too mad. I'll tell you after the game."

"Why do I think I'm taking the rap for whoever's pissed you off?"

"It's good for you to lose once in a while. It keeps you humble. Come on."

Back they went, and, as they'd both foreseen, Genna won, not with finesse or skill—she was totally outclassed by Marcy—but with pure, brute force. She felt strong enough to win an iron woman competition, and heaven help anyone who got in her way.

They both showered, changed and collapsed in the club lounge. Over juice and muffins Marcy raised an eyebrow. "So?"

Genna broke a bran muffin into seventeen pieces, didn't eat even one, then wiped her hands on her napkin. Even after an hour and a quarter of brutally beating on a little rubber ball she still felt sick with fury. "You know how I won that game?"

"Drugs?"

She shook her head. "I kept imagining Nick's face on the ball. Then I'd smash it as hard as I could."

Marcy sighed. "Oh, no. What's he done?"

The absolute enormity of his crime almost choked Genna. "You know my secret lover? The Friday-night guy?"

Marcy's face paled suddenly. She leaned forward and grabbed Genna's forearm. "Oh, my God. Nick found out about him?"

It was hard to get the words past her clenched jaw, but, like prisoners escaping, they managed to steal past her teeth. "Nick *is* him."

"What!" Heads turned as Marcy shrieked the question.

"That was Nick, all the time. My Friday-night mystery lover. It was Nick. Sneaking around pretending to be a stranger. Lying cheat. Bastard!"

"Wait a second. I don't even get this. Nick Cavallo? He was your mystery lover?"

She nodded, not trusting herself to speak.

"But...didn't you notice? Couldn't you tell?"

"No! It was always dark, one time he blindfolded me." She shut her eyes as a wave of humiliation washed over her. More than a wave—a tsunami. He'd blindfolded her and studied every inch of her naked body in the light. Not some anonymous fantasy stranger. It was Nick who'd seen her deepest secrets. Nick who'd made her lose control and cry out. He'd made her beg. She ground her teeth. "How was I supposed to recognize him?"

"I'm not sure." Marcy shrugged. "It's like me sleeping with Darren and not knowing it was him."

"I'd never slept with Nick before," she explained with deliberate patience.

"Well, I know. But didn't his hair feel familiar?" Marcy closed her eyes for a minute and a frown of concentration creased her brow. "Didn't you smell him? I could pick out Darren anywhere just from his smell."

"I don't spend a lot of time sniffing Nick. How would I know what he smells like? A rat. That's what he smells like. A dirty, stinking rat."

She thought about it for a second. "Anyhow, the guy in the hotel always showered. I'd get there and he'd be in a hotel robe, sometimes his hair was still wet from the shower." A smaller wave of anger swamped her. "Dirty manipulating cheat. I bet he showered deliberately so I couldn't smell him."

"Or maybe he was just being considerate, showering off the day's dirt before making love to you? I like that in a man."

"Then you should have hung on to him. Creep."

"Your affair's been going on for weeks. How did you find out the truth?"

This was the worst part. The part that made her want to put out a contract on Nick. Just when she'd begun to trust him... She dropped her forehead in her hands. "I told my Friday guy I couldn't see him anymore. Because I was getting involved with someone else."

"You mean...?" Marcy gasped and put a hand over her mouth.

"Yeah. Nick. I thought maybe I had a future with that bastard." Her eyes burned.

"You and Nick?" Marcy was almost jumping up and down with glee. "Honey, that's fabulous. He's perfect for you."

Genna raised her head just enough to glare. "There is no Nick and me. Soon there'll be no Nick. I'm putting out a contract on him."

"You mean a hired killer? Don't you think that's a little extreme?"

"Nick's Italian. He'll understand." She contemplated the picture for one satisfied moment. "Right before the bullet goes through his head, he'll know not to mess with me."

"I'm sure it's a mistake he won't make again," Marcy said on a half laugh.

Now that she'd started, the urge to unburden herself was too great to hold back the worst. "I thought..." She paused and swallowed, hating the way her voice had begun to tremble. "I told him I loved him."

"Who? Nick? You told Nick?"

"Not Nick. I mean, yes, Nick, but I didn't know it was him then. I told him I couldn't see him anymore because of this other guy that I was serious about." Her cheeks were burning. Now she wished she'd just kept her mouth shut. How much more humiliation did she have to wallow in? "And he asked me if I was in love with this other guy. And I said yes."

"What did he say?"

"That's when he turned on the light."

Dishes clattered from behind the swinging door that led to the kitchen. A pair of moms in tennis whites, with toddlers in tow, settled themselves at the next table chattering nonstop. But at Marcy and Genna's table there was silence.

Genna's throat was parched and she drained her glass of orange juice in one long, continuous swallow.

Marcy stared until her eyes bugged out. "And?" She all but yelled.

"There is no 'and.' I hit him and left."

A choked laugh came from her companion. "You *hit* him?"

"Not nearly hard enough."

"Then what?"

"Then I left."

"Did he try and stop you?"

Genna shook her head.

"Say anything?"

She glowered. "He said he loved me. Stinking weasel."

A glimmer that looked suspiciously like a hastily repressed grin crossed Marcy's face. "So, a man you're in love with turns out to be the fantastic lover you didn't want to give up. And he tells you he loves you. You know, there are worse things that could happen to a girl."

"You don't understand! He lied, cheated, deceived me. He controlled the whole thing and I—I—"

"Didn't." Her friend didn't even bother repressing the smile anymore. "For once in your life you weren't in control of everything. And it scared the hell out of you."

"That's not—"

"You need to decide what you're really mad about. You know commitment isn't your strong point. Maybe you need to think about that. About what you really want."

"I told him I hate him."

Marcy shrugged. "Love and hate are kissing cousins. You've got the rest of the weekend to sort your feelings before you see him on Monday. You might be surprised at what you find. And you know I'm just a phone call away." Marcy glanced at the noisy toddlers at the next table, then her eyes widened and she checked her watch. "Agh! I have to get home. Darren's got a basketball game. I promised I'd be home to take over the kids."

"Sure," Genna said. She was in a bit of a snit at the casual way her "friend" made light of Nick's huge betrayal. Making Genna think she might somehow be responsible. Some friend.

Marcy gave her a one-armed hug and a huge noisy smacker on the cheek. "Call me Monday."

"If I'm not in jail for murder."

Marcy's advice was absolutely terrible. Too bad she'd bothered to unload on her. Genna wanted female sympathy, a good bout of male-bashing and especially Nick-bashing. She did not need barely restrained giggles and a suggestion this was somehow *her* fault.

With friends like Marcy...

Scowling as she drove away from the health club, she reviewed her to-do list in her head. She might be deeply disturbed and in a crisis, but her list of jobs wasn't going to take a holiday. She stopped at the grocery store, picked up her dry cleaning and then, in a burst of self-pity, bought a bunch of tulips from the flower shop beside the dry cleaners.

After she got home, she unloaded her groceries, hung her clothes and found a vase for the bright red blooms. Only then did she allow herself to check her phone messages, ready to hit Delete the very instant she heard the rat-weasel's voice.

There were three messages. She rolled her eyes. The man was truly pitiful.

She listened to the first message. Her mother.

The second was from her dentist, reminding her of her scheduled six-month checkup the following week.

The final message was from the club informing her she'd left her racquet and sports bag in the coffee shop. She ground her teeth in annoyance. She never did stupid things like that.

NICK TAPPED his fingers against the phone, squinting with his good eye as he tried to work out the best course of action.

And action there would be. That he promised himself. Maybe he'd been foolish to expect Genna to leap into his arms the minute the light went on. He could have understood a few minutes of shock, maybe a tear or two.

But a black eye?

For what? What had he done but deliver her fantasy on a silver platter? Did she think it had been easy for him, sneaking around in the dark to service her, and then having to pretend when they saw each other every damn day at the office that he didn't know her body as well as he knew his own? That he didn't know the sound she made just before she peaked? That helpless little growling gasp just before she gave up control and let go?

Did she think he was just playing games with her? That hurt worse than his throbbing eye.

Did she think he didn't love her?

He tossed the phone aside. He had no intention of phoning so she could hang up on him, of groveling so she could shove his face in the dirt.

Genna was one screwed up lady. She wanted faceless, nameless sex and she got it. Great faceless, nameless sex in fact.

Then she wanted a relationship. No problem. Nick was happy to provide.

So why the hell didn't she want great sex with her relationship? Did she like eggs without bacon? Ice cream without chocolate sauce?

What was wrong with the woman?

And what was wrong with him?

He'd spent four years of his life lusting for her.

He stumbled into the bathroom to shower, wincing as, despite his best efforts, water sprayed his black-and-blue cheek and eye.

No. Not lust.

Lust he could get over.

He'd been in love with the woman from almost the first moment. Her impact on him had never been small, from the instant she smacked right into his heart to the moment she'd punched his lights out.

Well, this was it. Once and for all. Now or never.

He'd have one more shot at making her accept that she loved him right back, or he'd give up on the most stubborn, overcontrolled woman he'd ever met. Why, oh why, did it have to be Genna he'd fallen for?

He toweled off and then prepared to shave. Except his razor wasn't in the drawer where it should be. With a muttered oath he stomped back to his bedroom where he'd tossed his unused overnight bag from Friday. Retrieving the black bag from the corner, he upended it, scattering the contents on his bed. Condoms, toothpaste and extra toothbrush, his razor, the scented oil he'd never smoothed on her body, the scarf...

He picked up the wisp of silk and held it to his nose, catching a hint of Genna's scent. He'd never erase the image of her spread out on the bed, gloriously naked, panting with arousal and, in that moment, absolutely and completely his.

Black eye or no black eye, he wasn't finished with Genna yet. How to make her accept the obvious? That they were in love with each other? Meant to be. He'd played it badly and now she had all her defenses up.

He touched the silk to his black eye—and her offenses.

He needed a plan.

Picking up the razor he went back to the bathroom, thinking hard. He shaved as best he could, while he devised and rejected a dozen plans. A glimmer of an idea came to him as he was wiping away the last of his shaving cream with a hot wet towel. It wasn't brilliant, but it might just work.

He scribbled a few notes as he gulped coffee and the idea slowly became a plan.

It wasn't much of a plan. In fact it was as feeble as a grown man hiding in the dark having secret sex with a woman he'd known for years.

But it was the best idea he had. Damn he hoped it worked.

GENNA SCOWLED at her reflection in the steamy mirror. She looked like a wreck. And she certainly wasn't going to work looking like a woman who'd spent a miserable weekend. One who'd barely slept in two nights.

By the time she'd unearthed a cover-stick from her makeup drawer and drawn beige half moons over the dark rings under her bloodshot eyes, by the time she'd tried to cover the now beige-and-blue rings with foundation, by the time she'd gooped on gray eyeshadow to draw the observer's eye away from the bulging bags that looked like old-lady stage makeup under her eyes, and by the time she'd found some blush to give her pale face some color, the little clock stuck to the mirror told her she'd spent twelve extra minutes on her morning routine.

The navy blue suit she'd put out the night before made her look as if she was going to a funeral. No, she amended, turning critically before the full-length mirror. She looked like the one ready for burial.

She had to face Nick today and she'd be damned if she'd look downcast and more dead than alive.

She shoved the suit back in her closet, so distracted she hung it out of order, among the winter weight woolens. There must be something bright in here somewhere, she thought, as she pored through summer suits in beige, navy and white. She flicked through all her slacks and blouses—dull, dull, dull. Dresses—better. The navy linen she'd worn in the garden that first night. *Definitely not.* Mint-green silk. She held it against her and dashed to the mirror, and her lip curled.

Mother of the bride.

Dead mother of the bride.

Finally she grabbed a pale blue linen sheath that she hardly ever wore because it tended to crease. Hah, who was going to notice a crease or two when they could check out the set of matching luggage under her eyes? She added some chunky silver beaded craft-fair jewelry. She glanced longingly at the toeless sandals that she'd wear barefoot, but she couldn't do it. She left her panty hose on and slipped into cream low-heeled pumps.

As she locked the door behind her, she refused to glance at her watch. More bad news she didn't need. Instead, she started a pep talk that lasted all the way to the office.

I am a mature grown-up. I will treat Nick with

distant courtesy. No one will ever know he broke my heart.

She tried to prepare for the ordeal. Deliberately, she conjured his image, strolling into her office, his laundered shirt rolled at the sleeves, his tie partly loosened and pain stabbed her temples. "I hate you!" she yelled at the vision.

Tears burned her eyes and she had to pull over to calm herself. She decided to forego the distant courtesy bit and just avoid the creep.

Her heart was speeding and her scowl was on full alert when she reached her floor. She managed a few barely civil greetings on her way to her desk. Almost lost it when her secretary's eyes bugged then shifted to the clock.

"Morning," she grunted in a tone that really said, "You wanna make something of it?" then finally reached the sanctuary of her office.

Except her sanctuary had been desecrated. Invaded by the enemy.

He'd sent her a memo.

Their first communication since the man ripped out her heart and spat on it, and he was sending her a memo. She picked up the white paper in fingers that trembled. It wasn't even personalized, just a reminder memo of the meeting of all parties in the Ross case. She turned it over, her fingers leaving damp marks, unable to believe there wasn't some kind of message, an apology, something!

But the back of the memo was as pure white as a clear conscience. Something Nick certainly didn't have.

She stared at the brief reminder memo, let her eyes

linger on Nick's name at the top, let herself feel the pain of his betrayal. How he must have laughed at her all those weeks, enjoying his own private joke while she, the butt of the joke, had remained oblivious. She'd totally let herself go—God she cringed to think about it—precisely *because* he'd been a stranger.

If she'd known that was Nick there in the bedroom with her, well she never would have...

Slowly she slumped into her chair, feeling as though her legs couldn't hold her up anymore. She couldn't go to the meeting. She simply could not face the man. It was too soon, besides she felt a headache coming on, a sharp pain behind her eyes. She started typing an e-mail telling him she wouldn't be there, then paused, the arrow hovering over the send icon.

Only a coward would send that message.

She'd never been a coward, and no cheating scum was going to turn her into one. She'd go to that meeting. Her jaw tightened as she deleted her message. Distant courtesy, she reminded herself. She'd be purely professional—they had to work together after all. And instead of spinning fantasies around a man lower than a dung beetle, she'd utilize her energy more productively and redouble her efforts to become a partner before her next birthday.

Partner. She closed her eyes and pulled up the image that always inspired her to work harder, study longer. It was the picture of her own name on the firm letterhead. The partners' names were listed in order of seniority on the upper left of the letterhead, subtly and tastefully embossed. It was a symbol, like the window office and the partners-only meetings and dinners, that would mean she had done it. She'd arrived.

She saw the letterhead clearly in her mind's eye. There was her name, at the bottom of the list, true enough, but there, as a full-fledged partner. She drew a deep breath and waited for the warm flutter of excitement that fueled her ambition.

It didn't come.

She squeezed her eyes tighter and breathed deeply once more. Now she was shaking hands with the managing partner as he welcomed her to her first partners' meeting. There they all were, waiting to shake her hand and congratulate her. But she only saw one man.

Nick. He had the same intense expression on his face that he'd worn when light exploded in the hotel room Friday night. Eyes still closed, she tried to conjure the face of Betty Perkins, the first woman ever to become a partner. But Betty's face wouldn't appear.

Nick kept getting in Betty's way, walking relentlessly toward Genna with his hand out.

And the emotion she felt wasn't satisfaction.

It was fear.

She gasped and her eyes flew open.

Her heart was pounding and her palms damp. She was terrified.

That was ridiculous. Of course she wasn't frightened of him. It must be anger at what the jerk had done to her. Fear implied that she wasn't in control, and that was simply ridiculous.

She grit her teeth and consulted her Day-Timer for her most important task of the day. Then she got to work.

Her shared secretary buzzed her. "Genna, it's five to ten. Nick just rang and asked me to remind you."

"Thanks." She ignored Maureen's mildly puzzled tone. When had Nick ever had to remind her of anything?

Never.

And if he had something to tell her, he told her himself. He didn't use messengers.

Well, if that's how he wanted to play it. Fine. "Would you buzz his secretary back and tell her I'll be there."

"Sure…"

"Oh, and Maureen, do you have any pain relievers? I've got a headache."

"I thought you looked kind of sick when you came in. Yeah, I've got some stuff in my drawer."

"Thanks, I'll be right out."

Genna gathered her materials on the Ross case, grabbed a couple of pills and took a detour to the ladies' room. She filled her hand with water from the sink and swallowed down the pills, grimacing as they stuck just behind her breastbone.

Under the fluorescent lights the undereye concealer didn't seem to be doing such a terrific job. She dampened a finger and tried to smooth it a little, then dropped her hand with a huff of annoyance as the stuff caked. If she had time she'd just wash her face. But she didn't have time. "Hell with it," she muttered and stalked out.

Determined to ignore the nerves fluttering in her stomach, she sailed into the conference room, one calculated minute late, just to be certain she and Nick wouldn't have any time alone.

She was pleased to see Mr. Ross already seated, his lawyer beside him.

She greeted them both with a smile and a handshake, then her eye turned, almost involuntarily, to the head of the table where Nick sat.

A gasp escaped her. "Nick. Your eye!" Had she done that? It was swollen half-shut, a dark purplish-black bruise spreading from his eye to his nose and partway down one cheek.

The expression in his good eye was cynical. "You should see the other guy."

Her cheeks burned. She opened her mouth to apologize then shut it again. The last thing he'd want was for anyone to think he'd been beaten up by a girl.

Even though he deserved it, she hadn't meant to hit him so hard.

Mr. Ross said, "I caught a tennis ball in the eye once, too. Damn, it hurt."

"I remember asking you if it was a jealous husband who'd socked you one," came a soft voice from the doorway.

Mr. Ross half rose. "Tiffany." Genna glanced up to see the strong attraction between them, the forgiveness and hope pulling them together. It was so naked, she turned her gaze away.

Ross's lawyer cleared his throat, and Tiffany looked around. "Sorry I'm late. The kids wanted to finish a picture for Daddy."

"How are——" Ross began but was interrupted by Tiffany.

"Here it is." She leaned across the rosewood boardroom table and dropped the drawing in front of her husband. Artists these kids would never be, Genna decided, sneaking a peek at the crayoned image of a house, apple tree and some kind of black scribbled mass she assumed was the household pet. Mr. Ross had tears in his eyes when he glanced up at his wife, and oddly, Genna, who hadn't cried once all weekend, felt her own eyes prick with emotion.

"Thanks, Tiff," he said, his voice husky.

There was a pause. Nick broke it. "Good morning, Mrs. Ross. We're all here so let's begin. This is an informal meeting, but we can bring in a secretary to take notes if anyone feels that would be helpful?"

There was a general shaking of heads.

Nick nodded. "We're here to agree on a marriage counselor and set dates that work for both parties."

Genna didn't understand why they had to have this meeting in person; it sounded like a big waste of time to her. Nick and Mr. Ross's lawyer could have worked this stuff out on the phone. She calculated that the meeting would take about ten minutes. Fifteen if they had questions. She glanced at her watch. She'd be out of here by ten-fifteen at the latest. Sooner if she could speed things up.

She hated being in this room. Hated looking at Nick with his black eye and hard expression. Hated to the depths of her being that she'd lost both her fantasy lover and her best friend all in one go.

She'd expected Nick to try to get her back. All weekend she'd braced herself to hear his voice on her service, find him at her door, turn away huge bouquets of flowers.

It hadn't occurred to her that he might feel like the injured party. Or that he'd carry on as though nothing had happened. Business as usual, except from now on they'd communicate through their secretaries. Damn it, if he intended to treat her with distant courtesy, she didn't think she could bear it.

The headache was getting worse. All the pain reliever seemed to do was give the heartburn. She twisted her neck a little, trying to ease the pressure without drawing attention to herself, when Nick spoke again.

"Love doesn't always work out," he said in a soft voice that had her jerking her head back his way, eyes wide. Wasn't this meeting supposed to be about scheduling?

He was glancing from Tiffany to Rory Ross as he spoke, but Genna had a feeling he was speaking to her. She swallowed, trying to ease the heartburn that was getting more intense by the second.

"Sometimes the person we fall in love with isn't the person we're meant to be with, and ending it is the only sane solution. You can love someone and feel that they've grown so used to you that they don't see you anymore. I think that's how Tiffany was beginning to feel. Right, Tiffany?"

She nodded, black curls bouncing.

An awful pain started squeezing Genna's chest, just like the headache, only lower. What was he getting at? That he'd made a mistake getting involved with Genna?

"It happens all the time. We see people in a certain way and that's all we see. Whether it's as wife, friend, co-worker..." His glance just flicked on Genna and passed on. She didn't want to look at him, but she couldn't help herself. His voice was so solemn, his one good eye so clear and serious. His cheek was patchily shaved under his bad eye, as though it had hurt too much to press the razor.

''We sometimes become blind to them in any other role.''

Is that what had happened with her? Had Nick wanted to be more than friends but she'd been too blind to notice? They'd always been such good friends. Surely he hadn't wanted to spoil that special bond any more than she had.

Or had he?

They'd had all sorts of conversations over the years and she must have made her feelings pretty clear. She wasn't interested in romance. Only her career. She bit her lip, realizing how arrogant that must have sounded. And how blatantly untrue it had turned out to be.

She did want love. It didn't lessen her as a woman, or get in the way of her career. It enhanced her life. Added sparkle. Nick had taught her that.

''And sometimes the other person—the one who feels unseen, taken for granted—does something foolish,'' Nick continued.

Tiffany sniffed and Genna passed a full box of tissues. ''Tiffany was wrong to answer that personal ad. And she admits it.'' The dark-haired woman nodded, her head down, mouth hidden by a tissue.

''But there was a reason she acted the way she did. Why she did something outlandish to get your attention.

''Now it's up to you,'' he said to Mr. Ross, but again he glanced briefly at Genna. And there was no mistaking his message.

''Are you going to give her another chance? Do

you love her enough? Do you trust her enough? I've been in this business long enough to know that trust is the most important thing between two people. If you don't have that, you don't have anything. Before you decide how to proceed, I want you to think very carefully."

"I don't need to think about it," Mr. Ross said, his voice a trace husky.

Tiffany raised her head and the tears sparkling on her cheeks looked like Christmas tinsel.

"I'm no good with words and stuff, but he's right, Tiff. I—I guess I wanted the woman I married. Remember how much fun we had when we were just starting out? Then the kids came along and I guess I wasn't ready for everything to change. I could have helped more. I will help more. I want you back. I'll try harder this time."

"Me, too," his wife said, trying to wipe her eyes and blow her nose at the same time.

"All right," Mr. Ross's lawyer spoke up. "My client is willing to undertake marriage counseling. He agrees not to pursue a divorce at this time."

"Or any time," Mr. Ross said. "I was an idiot. I know you wouldn't go with another guy. I shoulda talked to you. I'm sorry."

Genna felt as if she were watching it all from far away. Tiffany and Rory Ross had children together and a marriage to save and she was so happy for them that they were working together for their future.

But was Nick trying to draw a parallel?

They had nothing at all in common with Rory and Tiffany.

Did they?

Tiffany had almost lost everything she loved most because of a fantasy. Genna had also been caught up in a fantasy. Except it hadn't been a fantasy, it had been a deception. Now Nick wanted to end the deception, he wanted Genna to trust him, to believe he loved her.

But how could she?

Questions plagued her. If Nick hadn't lied in word, he'd lied in deed, letting her believe... Oh, shit. She'd let herself believe exactly what she wanted to. And now she didn't know what to believe.

She snapped her binder closed when Rory reached a hand across the table to his wife. Genna glanced at Nick and found him gazing at her. It was all there for her to see in his one good eye. Love, pain, remorse, hope. Her own eyes filled; all she felt was confusion.

She couldn't stay here. She could not continue to sit in this room with the man she both loved and hated, her heart in such turmoil she could barely breathe.

She needed some air.

She stumbled to her feet. "Would you excuse me?" she said. "I've got another meeting." She managed a polite smile for Mr. and Mrs. Ross. "I'm so glad things are working out for you."

Then she grabbed her stuff and headed rapidly out the door. She hit the hallway and her knees sagged so she almost staggered.

"Genna." His voice was soft and low behind her.

She didn't turn around. Couldn't. She heard the appeal in his tone and knew if she looked in his face she'd lose it completely and throw herself at Nick, her lover, and sob her heart out against the chest of Nick, her friend.

But right now, Nick was neither her lover nor her friend. He was her enemy and she didn't trust him, or herself.

She flapped her hand over her shoulder. "I can't," she said. "Not now."

She started walking.

And kept on walking. She headed straight for the elevators, down to the main lobby and out into the bright sunshine. She blinked as the light almost blinded her, then dug in her bag for her sunglasses. Her escape was completely irresponsible. She had clients, work, but it didn't seem to matter. She had to get away and think.

If she could just *think.*

14

GENNA'S DRESS began to stick to her as she wandered aimlessly in the midmorning heat. Without conscious thought, she headed for the lakeshore, and somehow the noise and bustle of Navy Pier lured her. It was far away from her normal world, and just at the moment, that felt good.

Tour boats scooted across Lake Michigan, and she heard the odd tale of Chicago history and folklore. Even on the water she noticed how most of the tourists had huddled under the awnings out of the sun or viewed the sights from inside air-conditioned cabins.

Navy Pier was crowded with tourists, loafers, moms and kids, military types. She decided noise and bustle would help drown the ceaseless buzzing of confused thoughts droning in her head.

Her shoes pinched and her panty hose felt like woolen underwear. Everyone around her seemed to be having such a good time. They all seemed so relaxed, and she was almost positive she was the only one in panty hose.

She found a washroom and pulled off the offending nylons and stuffed them in her bag. Maybe she just needed a short break.

She wandered back out into the sunshine and sat on a bench. She leaned back, relaxing into it. She slipped off her shoes. Soon it became clear to her that she wasn't going back to the office. Not today.

She stared out at the huge gray lake, feeling her future stretch just as colorlessly before her.

Maybe she should leave Donne, Green and Raddison, move to a new firm, make a brand-new start.

Even as the thought occurred, anger unfurled like a big red hot-air balloon, filling her chest so she could barely breathe. It was so unfair of Nick. She'd never dated colleagues for this very reason. Breaking up meant nothing but horrible awkwardness and you still had to work with the person.

He was the one who should have to quit. She snorted. Like that was going to happen. *Nick Cavallo* was a partner. *Genna Monroe* was a mere associate. Pretty obvious which one would have to go.

She knew she was being unfair. Nick would do the right thing. She knew it as well as she knew this man who'd been her friend and mentor for four years. Her eyes prickled foolishly at the thought of never being friends again.

In fact, she experienced a double loss. It was still difficult to take in the fact that Nick and her secret lover were the same person. She felt that she was grieving both the loss of a friend and the loss of a lover.

Marcy's words from Saturday morning floated into her mind. "Having him turn out to be a great lover as well as a great friend isn't the worst thing that could happen to a girl."

Did she have to lose both her friend and her lover?

Again, that ripple of fear slid through her, stealthy

and deadly as a poisonous snake. But it was a fear she would have to face.

If she could talk it out, maybe she could make sense of her confused feelings. There was only one person she could speak to about this. She needed to explain it to Nick, to make him understand.

Taking a deep breath, she dug out her cell phone and dialed.

"Cavallo," he answered on the first ring, and she almost dropped the phone at the impact his voice had on her.

"I'm afraid," she admitted, her voice low.

"Genna? Where are you?" Instantly, his voice was full of concern. She imagined he'd sat up straighter, probably was at this moment grabbing a pen and a notepad.

She glanced around. "At Navy Pier. Outside a bargain T-shirt outlet." Her nose twitched. "And somewhere near a hot-dog stand."

"Don't move. I'll be right there."

"No! Don't do that. I just want to talk to you for a minute. Are you alone?"

"Yeah. Are you okay?"

"Yes." Lie of the century.

"I want to come and get you."

"No. This is easier if I can't see you."

"Like making love?" His voice was softly taunting. But before she could answer, he said, "I'm sorry. I shouldn't have said that. It's just that you're making me crazy."

She gripped the phone. "I know. You're making me crazy, too. Anyway, you're right. It is easier when I can't see you."

"What are you afraid of?"

"I just…I think about…being with you and it scares me."

She heard a short laugh. "It scares me, too. I could end up blind."

Her teeth sank into her lower lip as she recalled the shiner he'd sported in the meeting. "I'm sorry about that. I didn't mean to hit you so hard."

"No. It's my fault. I shouldn't have sprung it on you like that. I thought you'd be happy. Pretty stupid, huh?" She pictured him in his office, holding the phone in one hand. She could almost see him run his fingers through his hair like he did when one of them encountered a thorny problem and they talked it through.

"I'm just…I feel like you betrayed me. Why didn't you tell me it was you?"

"When?"

"I—"

"When would you have wanted to know?"

A seagull swooped down and pecked at a French fry somebody'd stepped on. Another, larger gull came at the first with a fierce squawk and they harangued over the pale white lump. She gripped the phone tighter, unable to answer his question. She'd loved the anonymity of making love with a complete stranger. Loved the seductive whisper and the possibility he could be the man of her dreams. Quite literally, in fact. The man no flesh-and-blood human could ever rival.

"The first time in New Orleans?" Was he whispering deliberately? She felt her body begin to tremble.

She was suddenly there, back in that darkened room where they'd first made love, the spicy-sweet scent of magnolia all around her. She'd never known a night like it. Would she have wanted to know it was Nick making her feel that way?

"I don't know," she answered at last, her voice husky.

"I offered to tell you my name that first night. Remember? You said you didn't want to know."

Now that was just plain unfair. "I know, but only because I didn't know it was *you!*"

His soft chuckle rumbled in her ear. "We'll let that obvious lapse of logic go. Are you sure you wanted to know?"

A child wandered by, dropping a trail of fragrant popcorn at her feet. He stared at her, obviously fascinated with her conversation and she dropped her voice as she replied, "I'm not sure of anything. I'm not sure I can trust you. That's why I'm scared."

"Bullshit." She pressed the phone tighter against her ear, but the child had already wandered on, and of course wouldn't have been able to hear the curse anyway. "You know you can trust me. It's yourself you can't trust. I had some time to think over the weekend. Me and my ice pack. You're scared of your own feelings."

Anger bubbled within her, stalled only momentarily by his referring to his ice pack. Damn, that eye really had looked sore. "Don't try to push this on me. You lied and...and...took advantage of me. Your lack of openness was in itself a deception."

"Never argue with a lawyer." He sighed. "I gave you your fantasy, Genna. I gave you what you wanted, all the time knowing I wanted more. I do want more. You were willing to end it with your fantasy lover so you could be with me. Don't forget that, will you? You chose me, Nick, with your eyes wide open.''

''But I—''

''I love you. Think whatever you need to think. You want to throw what we have away, that's up to you.''

''We don't have anything!''

A pause. ''If that's what you think, then we really don't have anything.''

She felt so miserable and confused, tears threatened. And that would never do. ''I have to go now,'' she said.

''Yeah. Me, too.''

And as she turned and faced her fear head-on, she knew why Nick frightened her. The same things that had drawn her to him as a friend terrified her as a lover. She loved his close family, the bonds he forged with his friends. His strength and focus. As a friend, they were wonderful qualities. In a mate they terrified her.

At last the tears began to fall.

Love was painful. She'd learned that lesson well. It was easy for Nick to talk about love with his big, traditional Italian family. They hardly ever got divorced. He couldn't know the pain of lost love as she'd seen it firsthand. The love that turned to bitterness then left the house altogether, leaving her feeling bereft and somehow guilty.

She'd learned to trust only herself, only what she

could control. It was so much easier to simply avoid the pain.

But then she was denied love's pleasures.

She wiped another tear. Her only alternative was to take the greatest risk of her life.

She sat up straight.

She'd never thought of herself as a coward before. And here she was, sniveling and whining because she might lose at love. She was so frightened to fail she'd given up without a fight.

Over? Was it over? She hadn't said half the things to Nick she wanted to. Furthermore, he hadn't groveled. He'd barely apologized.

Tears fell down her face faster than she could wipe them. Oh, she was so confused. Even her thoughts were out of control. Everything was. It was her worst nightmare come true.

She'd turned into an out-of-control control freak.

Since she'd given all her tissues to Tiffany Ross, she had to wipe her streaming eyes with her hands and sniff all the way home.

He'd said the words that struck terror into her deepest being. *I love you.*

And yet, under her tears, warmth bubbled like a secret hot spring.

It was all right for Nick to spout love words. He didn't understand what she'd been through, how vulnerable she'd been with him. *He'd* never been seduced in the dark by no more than a whisper. *He'd* never been loved to within an inch of his life by a secret lover in the deepest darkness. *He'd* never lain there, waiting, wondering what would happen next, what part of his body would be touched, caressed.

How could he possibly understand the depth of his betrayal if he'd never experienced any of that?

She gasped as an idea—a punishment really—so devastatingly perfect, hit her.

Maybe it was time Mr. Nick Cavallo got a taste of his own medicine. And she knew just who was going to play doctor!

Miraculously, her mood lightened.

He loved her.

She loved him.

But before she forgave him for his deception, she was going to make it abundantly clear that their relationship would be an equal one. He'd called all the shots in their love life so far.

Now, it was her turn to take control. And that, after all, was what Genna did best.

She dried the last of her tears, glanced at her watch and sprinted into action.

NICK DROPPED into bed, tired and dispirited. He'd given it his best shot. Now he had to admit defeat. Genna hadn't tried to contact him again today. He'd left a message on her service, suggesting dinner. No answer.

He'd stopped by her loft, but if she was home she didn't answer the door.

He'd paused at a florist but then drove on. Knowing Genna, she'd interpret flowers as an apology, and he wasn't apologizing for what had happened. Their affair had been the best time he'd ever had, and damn it, he knew it had been for Genna, too. Sex that good could not be one-sided.

Of course it wasn't. There'd been love between

them long before they made love; Genna had simply refused to acknowledge it. Until he'd openly given her his love. Then she'd knocked it back in his face.

He flicked off the late news he'd barely taken in, and settled down to sleep. His king-size bed seemed awfully empty tonight. It was crazy, he'd never made love to Genna in this bed, and yet he could see her there, feel her.

He bunched up the pillow under his neck and flopped onto his belly. She'd never been in this bed, and chances weren't looking good she ever would. He had to face it. It was time to accept defeat and move on.

Time to move on.

He was still thinking about that when he eventually fell asleep.

Hours later, he awoke with a jerk, his body stiffening as all his senses snapped to attention. He'd heard something—what?

Opening his eyes wide didn't help. He was almost certain he'd left the drapes open, but he must have drawn them since he couldn't see a damn thing. Even the glowing light on his clock was obliterated—maybe the power was out? Was it the sound of the appliances conking that had woken him?

Always a heavy sleeper, he had a hard time getting his thoughts to focus. It was easier to drift back to sleep.

And yet he couldn't shake the feeling there was another presence in the room with him. He breathed slowly, his ears straining for a sound, fists bunching as he prepared to tackle an intruder.

His nostrils quivered on a familiar scent—*magnolia.*

"What the—?"

"Tell me what you want," a soft female voice whispered into his ear. She was close, so close he could feel her warmth and smell the scent that drove him wild.

Heat flooded his body, as did a softer emotion. She'd come to him. In spite of her anger, in spite of her fear, she'd come to him. "You know what I want," he whispered back, settling back against the pillows, wondering just what was coming next.

"I'm going to make you beg." She enunciated each word in that crisp no-nonsense voice that always turned him on. She hadn't even bothered whispering, arrogant witch.

"What if I don't want to?" He taunted her right back, knowing she had the power to make him beg, and do pretty much anything else she dreamed up, probably within seconds.

"You'll do what you're told." This time she whispered, husky and soft so close her breath swirled in his ear.

She kissed him softly, her lips clinging, trembling with emotion—totally at odds with the tough gal talk. Then the mattress dipped as she crawled, warm and naked into his bed.

She'd come to him.

He smiled sleepily in the dark. "I love you."

"You'll be sorry."

Her lips caressed his chin, his neck, and then the sharp edge of her teeth bit his nipple.

"Never," he promised, shifting until he was flat on

his back and she could have her way with him. She took her time, kissing and caressing every blessed inch, as though there was all the time in the world, and his midnight visitor was determined to stretch out every second.

She thought she was torturing him, but he knew from experience that it was a double-edged sword. The longer she dragged out the foreplay, the more she'd suffer herself. He almost laughed as he heard her breathing change as she worked her way down his stomach licking and teasing him. Twice he tried to touch her, first her breasts, then her hips, both times she pushed his hands back down to his sides.

Then she took him in her mouth and he forgot he had hands.

He couldn't take much, and she seemed to sense that. She came back up the bed and kissed his mouth, long and deep. She shifted and he felt one knee brush his abdomen as she settled over him. Just at the brink where she was so hot and so wet, he felt her rub his hardness, but she didn't take him into her body, just paused there for a second.

He felt her body shift slightly and he wondered if she was going to his bedside table for a condom.

With a snap, the bedside lamp burst into light, making him jump with the shock. He squinted at the unexpected brightness, then gazed into her face as understanding dawned.

She was bringing their relationship into the light.

He watched her face as he'd wanted to do so many times while they'd made love. He touched her cheek, where her fair skin glowed gold. Then their gazes connected…and he felt more naked than he'd ever felt in his life.

Vulnerable. Open. Connected, but not yet all the way. He gazed at her breasts, puckered and hard-tipped, rising and falling with her rapid breathing.

"Why did you come back?"

Her eyelids were puffy so he knew she'd cried earlier, but now her eyes glowed with the same emotion that he felt glowing inside him. "I decided the payoff was worth the risk." She bit her lip and met his gaze with her own. "Maybe it won't work out," she said softly, running a hand through his hair. "But maybe it will."

"I will always love you," he promised, knowing it was true, and if it took him all his lifetime he'd prove his love and fidelity to the most stubborn woman God ever created.

He gazed down her flat belly to the triangle of dark blond curls. A drop of moisture pearled at the pink tip of flesh just peeking out. His own much larger flesh waited impatiently at the entrance to her body.

"I love you, too," she finally admitted and lowered herself onto him, taking him deep inside her until they were truly as connected as two people can be.

He gazed up to find her eyes watching him, bright with tears.

"It's like the first time," he whispered, amazed at how much love they were making just with eye contact. Amazed at how different it was in the light, both of them knowing whom they were with.

"It is the first time. As us."

"No more disguises," he agreed, lifting his hips

greedily, trying to fill her fuller, penetrate her deeper than he ever had before.

"No more hiding," she admitted on a gasp.

"Still scared?"

"Terrified."

"Me, too."

Then she began to move on him. Slowly at first, as they let their eyes feast on each other and the sight of their joined bodies, hers so fair and milky, his darker and hairier.

"Lean back," he begged her, greedy to see everything. She did, arching her spine until she rested on her hands and they could both watch, watch as the tempo increased, watch their faces as they became more focused. He could see the effort it cost her to expose herself like this, knowing it was him. Watched her eyelids flutter shut.

He held himself back, watching the pressure mount within her body. "Let go," he said, not whispering but using his own voice. "Look at me and let go."

She whimpered and he thought she wouldn't, then her eyes opened and she stared right into his eyes. He saw her suck her breath in sharply, watched her pupils dilate. He felt the squeezing and trembling in her body and knew he couldn't hold off much longer.

He reached his hand between their bodies and touched her, just the way he knew she liked to be touched. And, staring into his eyes, letting him see right inside her heart, she exploded, just as he exploded within her.

"Nick!" she cried out, pushing forward to wrap her whole body around and against his, and he thought his name had never sounded so good.

Later, as they lay collapsed and sated in his bed, he said, "I thought I'd lost you."

She traced her fingers lightly through the hair on his chest. "I thought about what you said. I'd already chosen you, as yourself. I guess I was looking for excuses to run. You were right about me. What I can't control, I avoid."

"You don't need to be scared. I won't take your independence, I won't get in the way of your climb to the top."

"I know," she said softly. "Anyway, I hear it's lonely at the top. I'm not going there alone."

"You don't have to," he promised, taking her to the top once more, up and over.

"You know," he said, when he got his breath back, "I must be crazy. I swear I smell magnolias."

She rubbed her cheek against his chest. "I called six florists and couldn't find any fresh ones. But I found some magnolia-scented body lotion. I rubbed it all over my body.

"Which reminds me," she propped herself up on one elbow to stare down at him, a crease between her brows, "where did you manage to find fresh magnolia every Friday night?"

He grinned and jumped naked from the bed. He strode to the window, pulled the drapes and opened the balcony door, hoping none of the neighbors were awake at four in the morning. He grunted as he hauled in the magnolia bush he'd had shipped from Louisiana. "I have my own supply."

She slid out of bed, her face beaming as she knelt beside him. "Oh, look," she said, reaching into the glossy green leaves. "Here's a brand-new bloom, just starting to open."

"Now how symbolic is that?"

He reached forward and she met him halfway, their lips meeting over the magnolia.

More fabulous reading from
the Queen of Sizzle!

LORI
FOSTER

with

Forever and Always

Back by popular demand are the scintillating stories of
Gabe and Jordan Buckhorn. They're gorgeous, sexy
and single…at least for now!

Available wherever books are sold—September 2002.

And look for Lori's **brand-new** single title,
CASEY in early 2003

HARLEQUIN®
Makes any time special®

HARLEQUIN®

Duets™

"EXCELLENT! Carol Finch has the ability to combine thrilling adventure and passionate romance into her long line of masterful romances that entice readers into turning the pages."

"A winning combination of humor, romance...."

–Romantic Times

Enjoy a
DOUBLE DUETS
from bestselling author
Carol Finch

Meet the Ryder cousins of Hoot's Roost, Oklahoma, where love comes sweepin' down the plain! These cowboy bachelors don't give a hoot about settlin' down, but when a bevy of strong-willed women breezes into town, they might just change their minds. Read Wade's and Quint's story in:

Lonesome Ryder?
and
Restaurant Romeo
#81, August 2002

HARLEQUIN®
Makes any time special®